AMIAYA ENTE

Presents

I Ain't Mad At Ya

A NOVEL

by

TRAVIS "UNIQUE" STEVENS

Copyright © 2005 by Travis Stevens

Written by Travis Stevens for
Amiaya Entertainment LLC

Published by Amiaya Entertainment LLC

Cover design by Marion Designs

Printed in the United States

Edited by Antoine "Inch" Thomas
ISBN: 0-9745075-5-5

[1. Urban-Fiction 2. Drama-Fiction 3. Harlem-Fiction]

Acknowledgements

Extra thanks goes out to Amiaya Entertainment (Tania & Inch) for helping me sharpen my vision and complete part of my mission. I wish you all the success and happiness in the world. I respect that you're doing your thing. I know one day Amiaya Entertainment will be running this Urban Novel business, like Def Jam is running the music industry.

I give thanks to my mommy, Grace, my sis, Boosie, my poppy, Hank, and everyone in the Hall family.

Shout out to my cousin Kountry in Beaumont, Texas, hold your head, we're in the same fight, just a different round. We'll paint the town in a minute.

To all my homies in Butner, NC, Big Whop, Sadiq, Nino (A.K.A) Little Vicious, Smoke Black, Little Shawn, Righteous with the mole on his nose, and A.B. My peoples in Fort Dix, NJ, Red, Pop (A.K.A.) Big "G". My homies in Lewisburg, Whiz, B-Dub, Big D (A.K.A.) Corporate America, TrueWear, Polo and the Entire Harlem World.

What up to my street team in New Haven, CT, Wilson. Raleigh, Durham, NC, Chris, Black and Big Egypt. I can't forget all the shorties that tried to do this bid with me but failed. I ain't mad at ya. If it wasn't for y'all, I wouldn't have seen the arms of my B.M., and last but not least, to all the God's in the Heavens and the Earth, Stay up.

Dedication

I would like to dedicate this book to my two angels, Shai and Morgan, plus my B.M., Toni. Thanks for keeping me grounded and putting up with my Aquarian ways and also for keeping my two angels focused and determined to be beautiful, successful women.

When times are rough, you always place your finger under my chin and lift up my head. When tears drip from my eye, you wipe them away and provide me with a shoulder to cry on. I know sometimes we have our differences, but we share the same vision and mission, so I know the love and respect we have for one another, as well as our children, will get us over the top. Just remember my motto, "Stay sharp and keep your vision clear."

"One Love."

Chapter 1

"It's raining. We should wait and do it another night," Freedom suggested. He was crouched low in the passenger seat of a dark blue Porsche that his partner in crime, Havoc, had stolen the night before from Garden City, Long Island.

Havoc, tucked beside Freedom in the driver's seat, took long slow pulls on a blunt of purple haze marijuana that Freedom had rolled while the two intently watched the location. It would be their first heist together.

"Hell no! We gots to do it tonight. Do you know how much money is in that building? That bread will feed your family *and* mines for a long time," Havoc explained.

Havoc and Freedom were street niggas that were getting a little paper but nothing in large sums like the one they expected to take during the evening's caper.

"Fuck it. Let's get this money then," Freedom sounded excited to the point where Havoc could sense it in his voice. He was also nervous but he would never let Havoc witness that side of him.

Havoc kept his focus and attention on the building, took another drag on the blunt and, in a raspy voice said, "That's what I'm talking about," as he blew the smoke out slowly.

Then he thought to himself, *A hundred thousand dollars! If this goes as planned, I'll be able to invest in my construction business.*

"I'ma drive the car back to the stash spot. By the time I get there, you should have already done what you had to do. If there are any problems, hit me on the cell."

Havoc would let Freedom do the easy *breaking and entering shit.* But when it came time for the gunplay, Havoc would be on the front line calling *and* licking all the shots.

Freedom looked on as he grabbed the blunt for his last pull. He inhaled, then offered the weed to Havoc who declined by shaking his head. Freedom then reached for the ashtray and stubbed the blunt.

"I'll meet you at your crib in an hour, ah-ight?" Havoc said. He was looking over the spot one last time hoping that everything would go right. He needed that money. The streets were beginning to catch up to him and he felt it was time to chill out. The construction company would do him hell-a-good if everything jumped off the way it was supposed to.

Havoc placed his foot on the clutch and the brake, and put the brand new sports car into first gear. The duo proceeded with their customary handshake that always ended with a snap of their fingers, and before Freedom could exit the vehicle, Havoc added, "Yo, don't fuck me, Free." The look in Havoc's eyes told his partner in crime that he meant every word he said.

Freedom pulled his knitted hat low and tight to protect himself from the pouring rain, then stepped out of the car and ran, dashing through the puddles until he reached the building.

Havoc waited until he saw Freedom at the back of the building, then he skated off in his coupe.

Freedom entered the building through the basement doors.

Just as Havoc described it, it was there. In a dark corner of the basement sat a three-foot safe. Before Freedom proceeded to the safe, he reached into his book bag, pulled out a flashlight and gently let the basement doors close behind him. He directed the flashlight toward the safe's combination lock. As he punched in the numbers, he listened to every click, then he pulled on the handle and it opened. The money was all wrapped up in plastic zip lock bags. Nervous, he quickly but quietly placed all the stacks into the Ralph Lauren book bag that he had brought along with him. He placed the book bag on his back, dashed out the basement doors letting them close softly behind him. Freedom raced up the block and waited anxiously until he saw a taxi. He flagged the cabi down, and when it stopped for him, he opened the door and hopped in. Sweating profusely, Freedom wiped his brow and sank himself deep into the seats of the livery cab. Once he reached his apartment building, he gave the taxi driver a crisp twenty dollar bill and said to him, "You can keep the change." The Pakistani cab driver smiled, told Freedom to have a nice day and when Freedom was on the first step of the stairs that led to the entrance of his building, Habeeb drove off mumbling to himself, "Damn hoodlum."

Freedom reached his apartment, saturated from the pouring rain. Anxiously, he pulled the soaked book bag off of his back hoping that none of the money had gotten wet. Freedom pulled each stack of money out of the concealed zip lock bags. He quickly counted out ten thousand dollars. Once he was done, he tucked it into a hole in his mattress that he had previously made as a money stash.

An hour had soon passed when his cell finally rang. Immediately, he pressed the talk button. "Speak to me," he commanded.

"Let me in," Havoc yelled through the phone. His tone of

voice told his buddy that he didn't trust him.

Freedom buzzed him in and Havoc ran up the seven flights until he reached Freedom's door.

"Come in. I got it," Freedom smiled. He showed Havoc the money he pulled from his hiding spot. He dumped the thousand dollar stacks all over the floor.

"Roll this while we count," Havoc said as he threw Freedom a small plastic bag containing marijuana. Freedom rolled the joint and afterwards, the duo counted the hundred dollar bills and re-wrapped them into thousand dollar stacks. When they finally counted the last stack, Freedom gazed at Havoc trying to see his friend's reaction to only counting out ninety thousand dollars. Havoc looked up with his head slightly tilted to the side, with one eye open as he dodged the smoke from the blunt. He said, "It's ten grand short. You sure you didn't drop any of the money?" Havoc was told that it was gonna be a hundred grand in that safe, nothing more and *certainly* nothing less.

"That's all that was there" Freedom said convincingly!

Nervous, but calm, his expression seemed sincere, so Havoc continued on.

Havoc dumped the ashes from the almost finished blunt and began to explain. "So we got to split it 45-45, unless you're going to hit me off with my extra five?" Havoc was testing Freedom again, but Freedom kept his composure.

"Yo, I wouldn't beat you. If I was going to beat you, I wouldn't even be here talking to you," Freedom responded as he grabbed the blunt with his thumb and index finger.

Havoc realized that he had been beat, however, he reluctantly sat back and agreed. "Maybe the source was wrong," he said to Freedom. He figured getting forty-five thousand dollars from someone he barely knew was alright with him. He continued, "Yo, Free, I'm about to ditch this car, hop on the D-train and head back to Brooklyn." He placed his half of the money back into the wet book bag. He gave Freedom the customary handshake and ended it as usual with a snap of the fingers. They clutched as Havoc spoke.

"I'll hit you in about a week. We'll be going to Connecticut," Havoc said. This time he held Freedom's hand a half of a second before they snapped.

"Peace, kid," Freedom replied as he closed his door, locked it and placed the chain lock on the door as well. He quietly went back into the room, flipped the mattress over, found the hole and tucked the forty-five thousand along with the other ten thousand dollars back into it. He thought to himself, *This is the most money I have ever seen. I wonder what I should buy? How much should I save and how could I keep this money coming.* Freedom wasn't as talented as Havoc was with the stock market and business, but he did want to invest his money.

The next morning at around 7 a.m., Freedom counted out twenty thousand, put the rest back into the hole in his mattress and headed uptown to Broadway.

Chapter 2

Havoc and Freedom first met on the train about a month prior to the heist. Freedom was on his way home from an outstanding weekend with his female friend, Mercedes. He had on a 1988 black velour Gucci suit with the throw back Gucci sneakers and a big Cuban link chain with an enormous Jesus medallion with diamonds trimmed around the edges. His 38-inch chain hung low and sank into his Gucci patterned jacket. As he got closer to his stop, from his peripheral, he noticed someone watching him. Havoc was wearing a tailormade Prada shirt with black slacks, red suspenders and black Chelsea boots that Bally's had made back in the days.

At the time, Havoc was coming from Wall Street where he had just invested a couple of grand into a few Microsoft stocks. At that moment, Havoc realized that Freedom would be perfect for helping him along on his heists. As he flipped his fingers through the pages of the *Wall Street Journal*, he peered over the top of the newspaper. He squinted his eyes as he studied his target.

Freedom was nervous. He was looking out of the corner of his eye in Havoc's direction. He finally reached his stop, *142nd Street and Malcolm X Boulevard*. Freedom raced off the train. He was from the hood. He could always tell when some-one was scheming.

At first, he thought Havoc might be a stickup kid, then he figured he might be a cop looking to arrest him on some old charges. Havoc quickly raced off the train and followed behind Freedom. The two dashed through the terminal, one following the other out onto the streets. Havoc was walking quickly behind Freedom. As Freedom carried on, he continuously turned to watch his back. Then Havoc surprised him and yelled in an excited but exhausted manner. "Yo, let me get at you for a second." He continued to scream and wave his hand as if to say, "Come here!"

Freedom stopped, turned around and walked back down the block to Havoc's direction. He pointed at himself with a confused look and asked, "Are you talking to me?" Freedom was shaken, but he was trying to remain calm and not appear nervous.

Havoc assured Freedom that there would be no problems by reaching into his shirt pocket and pulling out a business card. He handed the card to Freedom, fell back and crossed his arms.

"What's popping?" Freedom asked. He struck a match and put one hand over his cigarette to block the wind from blowing the flame out.

"I have an offer for you that you won't be able to refuse. I have this situation and I need someone of your caliber to help me pull it off. It'll earn you fifty thousand dollars." Havoc began to explain to Freedom every intricate detail about the heist that would change both of their lives forever. Havoc waved his hand in a back and forth motion, protecting his nose from the Newport smoke and said, "I can't stand the smell of ciga-rette smoke." Havoc hated to be around people when they puffed on cigarettes; the odor from the tobacco irritated him. But let someone spark up an *"L"*, Havoc wouldn't mind being stuck in an elevator with a pack of Rasta Farian's holding a pound of weed, ten lighters and a box of Dutch's.

"Oh, I'm sorry," Freedom replied. He stubbed out the cigarette.

Havoc continued on about the issue that would soon change their lives and Freedom reluctantly agreed to everything that was said. "I'm in. When do we start?"

The two agreed to meet at a later date to go over the time and location of their up and coming caper.

Chapter 3

Freedom got off the train at 145th Street and Broadway. He paused and stared at all the beautiful Spanish women that passed him by. "Mi da, Momi," he yelled, trying to tighten up on his Spanish skills. Freedom tried to get the attention of a dark skinned lady who kept her eyes straight as she passed him. Unfortunately, his attempt ended up with negative results. Freedom stood in front of McDonald's until it was okay to cross the street. He entered a clothing store on the corner of 145th and Broadway and scanned the area. He was fascinated by all the Gucci, Prada and all the other designer names that were on the racks. There was one outfit that caught his eye, a grey and red velour Prada suit. Freedom walked over to it and looked at the hefty price tag. It read four hundred and fifty dollars for the pants, and the jacket was five hundred and seventy-five dollars. He quickly yelled out to one of the store-owners. "How much could I get the pants and jacket for?" Freedom looked around and hoped someone heard him. The store's owner looked at Freedom and as he responded, his facial expression was as if he had seen a ghost.

"Yo! Say it ain't so. I know that's not Free," the dude said. Before Freedom could say anything, he noticed it was

Memo. "Should I call my wolves, or should I lay you down and take every dime you got on you?" Memo said while he rubbed both of his hand together. Memo was dead serious too.

Memo was a caramel complexioned, Dominican dude about 35 years of age. He was known for having the best cocaine in the area. Anywhere between 140th and 145th streets around Broadway Avenue, you could find Memo hanging out with his wolves, or either managing his many clothing and sneaker stores.

One afternoon, a few months back, Freedom, who was a petty, *in the way hustler*, only known for copping ounces, decided to save up his earnings and head uptown to Broadway to cop a pie. Armed with only half of the money that it would cost to buy the whole kilo of coke, Freedom knew he would have to run the best of game to pull it off.

Memo, and a few of his wolves were standing in front of one of Memo's stores, when Memo noticed Freedom walking back and forth up the block. He motioned to one of his wolves to pay attention to Freedom. Then with a curious tone he said, "Go see what this kid is up to."

"Aight". One of Memo's soldiers replied. As the soldier approached Freedom, he looked Freedom up and down, motioned with his hand directing Freedom inside of nearby alley and said, "Yo, Papi, I got it for 28."

Freedom analyzed the soldier for a moment then asked in an excited tone, "What you got, fishscale?"

"Yeah." The Dominican man nodded.

"Well, a nigga only got 10 grand, but if you throw me something, I'll be sure to return." Freedom, said as he glanced at the soldier.

The soldier motioned with his index finger and said, "Wait

right here, I'll be back." Fifteen minutes later the soldier came back with his Boss, Memo, and introduced him to his new customer. Memo, looked at Free, glanced at his worker, then stated, "I'll throw you an extra 300 grams, and you'll owe me ten thousand dollars," Memo looked at Freedom, then locking eyes with him, he asked, "How long will it take you?"

"One week at the most," Freedom, figured. He watched every car that passed by the alley. At that point he realized his plan had worked. He shrugged his shoulders then stretched his hands and fingers, as if to say, *what are you waiting for?* Then he questioned. "So what's popping?"

"Ahight, Ahight, just don't make me come looking for you." Memo reluctantly agreed. With a puzzled look on his face he turned toward his soldier and with a simple wave of the hand, he motioned to his worker to hand Freedom the package. Freedom grabbed the bag of uncut raw cocaine, turned, smiled, balled up his fist then gave Memo a pound.

Freedom, proceeded back up the block. He hopped on the train, headed to his number one fiend's crack house.

Freedom hustled for days until he collected enough money to pay Memo back. When he paid Memo his money he instantly gained Memo's trust. He did this for a few weeks until he was given 500 grams on consignment. After a few heated dice games, one after another, a lack of budgeting and extensive shopping habits, Freedom was unable to hold up his end of the verbal contract between him and Memo. He was forced into hiding until he made his first heist with Havoc and trimmed the ten thousand dollars off the top of the one hundred thousand dollar caper. "Wait, wait," Freedom shouted, as he held the Prada suit and walked towards Memo. He began to explain with a lump in his throat. "I came out here only because I knew I would see you. I ran into a couple of prob-

lems. I caught a case, and I used the money to get out of jail."
Freedom was trembling and Memo noticed it.

"Do you expect me to believe that bullshit?" Memo
screamed at the top of his lung. He walked from behind the
counter. The store was empty, so no one witnessed Freedom
bitching up.

"Yo, Bee, I got the bread on me now," Freedom offered as
he reached for his pockets to show Memo what he was holding.

"Follow me," Memo stated and guided Freedom to an
empty storage room occupied by one lonely chair and like a
dozen empty boxes.

"I have the ten thousand dollars with me that I owe you,
plus I need another joint, but this time, a whole pie," Freedom
tried to explain. He looked Memo in the eye to show he was
serious.

"If you don't have fifteen thousand dollars, get the fuck
outta my face!" Memo yelled. Memo wanted to shoot Freedom
because he felt he was playing him, but he loved the money
Freedom was bringing in so he let him slide.

Memo reached for his little wooden chair and took a seat.
Freedom had something to prove. He pulled out the wad of
money that was wrapped in rubber bands and separated the
money into thousand dollar stacks.

Memo saw the money and said, "Okay, I'll give you a thousand grams, but I'm only giving you three days to come up
with my money," Memo stated in a low tone of voice. He
looked at Freedom with a raised eyebrow and continued. "If
you don't have my money, I'm gon' wire your lunchbox and
bury your ass wit' no casket. Now play yourself again." Memo
assured Freedom that this time around he wouldn't be so easy
going as before.

"So I guess I'll have fifteen thousand for you in three days," said Freedom. His eyes were wide. Never had he been in this type of bind before. He also knew just what block he would use to pump his product on.

"Meet me back here in thirty minutes," Memo told Freedom.

The two then walked toward the front of the store together. Freedom left the store, headed back up the crowded block and looked in storefront windows until he saw a diamond bezeled Frank Mueller watch on display that he always wanted. He dashed into the store and inquired to whoever was listening about the watch.

"How much does that watch cost?" Freedom was glowing. He was like a little kid in a candy store on allowance day.

"Seventy-five hundred," a store clerk said as she approached Freedom. She held her hand out then continued. "Hi, my name is Connie. Would you like to buy or put on lay away?"

Freedom shook the lady's hand and said, "I would love to buy it, but my money is kind of funny," Freedom joked as he looked the beautiful Dominican lady up and down.

"With twenty-five hundred, you can put it on lay away," Connie tried to get a sale on the watch. She gave Freedom a beautiful smile as she retrieved the paperwork from behind the counter so he could fill out.

"Ah-ight, I can handle that, and I'll be back next week to pick it up." Freedom filled out the proper paperwork, dug inside of his pocket and counted out twenty-five hundred dollars. He glanced at the time and realized he had to get back to where Memo was waiting for him. He left the store as soon as the lady showed him where to sign.

"I see you made it back," Memo said as he guided Freedom back to the dusty storage room.

"Do I need my scale?" Freedom asked in a sarcastic manner, then looked at is compadre.

"If it's not all there, we'll make it up later," Memo answered, then gave him the Prada suit he wanted and a heavily wrapped package inside of a shopping bag.

"In three days," Freedom reminded him, as he exited the storage room.

He left the store and as he waited for a taxi, he thought to himself, *I have thirty-five thousand dollars and a kilo. I can see thirty-five grand off of this key. If I break it down into ounces, then pay Memo his fifteen thousand, I can walk away with fifty-five grand.* He was brought back from outer space when a dirty Jamaican dude with dreadlocks stopped in a yellow cab and asked, "Where ya headed, dred?"

"A hundred forty-second street and Lenox Avenue," Freedom responded. He stepped into the back seat, clutched the shopping bag tightly and crouched low in the dirty cab. As they came up Lenox Avenue, Freedom watched every block, 140th, 141st, then 142nd. He paid the taxi driver, got out of the cab and looked up and down 142nd until he saw his man B.G., which stood for Body Guard. B.G. was an ex-kingpin who got strung out on his own supply of heroin and crack back in the late 80s.

One day back in 1988, B.G. and his partner in crime, a dude name Mike, sat low in B.G.'s 1988 silver colored Sterlin with some chrome B.B.'s rims to match. B.G. glanced at his rolex watch to check the time and said, "Damn, these bitches need to hurry up."

Mike looked at his partner, and spoke in a loud whisper, "Shit, Big Daddy kane probably won't perform until late anyway."

"This might be them bitches now," B.G. reached down and grabbed his sky pager from his hip when he felt it vibrating.

"Who is it?" Mike questioned, he leaned over the center console and looked at B.G.'s pager.

"Yeah, its them." B.G. assured. He sounded excited. He searched his astray, grabbed a handful of change, exited the vehicle, turned to close the door, proceeded to the payphone, inserted two dimes, then dialed the number that was on his pager.

Ring, Ring.

"Hello," Lois answered, she motioned with her hand to her best friend, a lady named Berniece, to past her the mirror that was covered with tiny lines of powder cocaine.

"What's up baby?" B.G. sounded upset, he stood at the payphone and looked back continuously at Mike who sat patiently in the car. "Are y'all still trying to go to the concert or what?" He questioned.

"Yeah, but its wack to be the first ones there." Lois explained, she dipped her pinkie nail into a stack of cocaine, titled her head, raised her finger to her nose and snorted one of the lines. Her eyes rolled into the back of her head and instantly became watery from the hit she just took. She continued. "So we'll go a little later, come through and have a few drinks"

"Ahight." B.G. relunctly agreed. He hung up the payphone, got back inside of his car then the duo proceeded to Baisley projects. The duo exited the car, entered through the building's doors and walked up four flights of stairs until they reached the girls apartment. B.G. politely knocked on the door.

"Who is it?" Berniece asked. She switched her small frame over to the door, stood on her tip toes and looked out the peep hole. When Berniece recognized who the men were, she opened the door.

"What's up with you, baby?" B.G. questioned as he entered

the apartment with Mike in tow.

"Yo, y'all not ready yet?" Mike asked looking at the females. "Shit, I'm not trying to miss Kane for nothing". The sound of his voice told the women that he wasn't feeling the environment. Mike was from Harlem but found himself lamping in a rough hood of the infamous Queens borough.

"Chill out, and stop tripping. Here, sip on this". Lois, smacked her lips and wiggled her head. She placed her hand on her hips then she continued, "Take a few lines of this powder to the brain, then you'll understand why Kane said *it aint no half stepping."*

"Take a few lines?" Mike recited what Lois said out loud. With a confused look on his face he sat next to B.G, grabbed the half full, crown royal bottle then took a quick swig. He twisted the top back on, then passed it to his partner in crime, B.G. B.G accepted the bottle, twisted the cap back off, took two quick swigs and as he swallowed he frowned his face up, as if he had stepped into a pile of horse shit.

The duo sat back on the couch and watched Berniece as she dug her pinkie finger nail into the powdery substance. She took a quick sniff, turned, looked at B.G. and Mike, wiped her nose with the tip of her thumb, and with tears in her eyes persuaded her male friend to ride the white horse with her. "Go ahead, get your mind right, it won't kill you."

B.G. grabbed the glass mirror. He didn't have any nails so he reached into his pocket, pulled out a one hundred dollar bill from the top of his wad of money, rolled it up, placed one tip on his nose and the other on the straight line of coke and reluctantly snorted the entire line. He caught a rush from the product, shook his head two quick times, caughed, and with tears in his eyes, he laid back on the sofa while Mike watched.

Mike did the exact same thing but when the duo came back

from their outta space mission, they joined a new team of play-
ers, and the coaches' name was Scotty. Scotty's favorite play to
run was *Beam me up*. The last thing the duo remembered was
1988 and Big Daddy Kane performing at the Latin Quarter's
night club. Up to this very day it's all they talk about when
they get up and go outta space.

"Yo, B.G., what's popping?" Freedom shouted as he jogged
up to the building B.G. was standing in front of. The two
greeted one another with a hand shake and a hug.

"Where have you been Big Free?" B.G. asked, while he
wiped the morning sleep away from his eyes and stretched.

"Just cooling, kid. I got some shit I need to whip up and get
out on the block," Freedom said in a serious tone of voice.

"Come in, let me see what you working with." B.G.
sounded excited. He guided Freedom through the doors, and
up six flights of stairs until he reached his apartment.

"Damn, B.G., you never clean up this place," Freedom
stated. He stepped over all the clothes and dirty blankets that
lay all over the small studio apartment.

"I had an exclusive party last night, kid," B.G. replied. He
quickly started gathering up the messy blankets. He threw them
into an empty hall closet.

"Yo, do money still be coming on this strip like before?"
Freedom asked as he lit up a cigarette. He dumped the match
into the ashtray and blew out a small cloud of smoke.

"It's still money coming through, but this kid, Trey, got it
on smash. He got a spot on 139th, so people go and see him
now," B.G. explained.

Freedom cleaned out a pot, reached into the shopping bag
and pulled out the package. He unwrapped the paper bag and
broke a small piece off of the hard white powdery substance.
B.G. pulled out his glass pipe. His body shuddered because he

was fiending for a hit of the cocaine. He trembled. "Damn, kid, that's a lot of coke, and that shit looks like fishscale." B.G. was looking at the work as if it was a naked lady.

"I'm gonna whip up a couple of grams and bag up a few eight balls," Freedom said as he prepared the temperature on the stove. He placed a few grams of cocaine and baking soda inside a jar, then gently lowered the jar into the boiling water until the cocaine became liquid form. For the next fifteen minutes he worked his magic and turned a thousand grams of cocaine into twelve hundred grams of crack.

"Yo, that shit came back like a mutha fucka. Let me take a hit," B.G. requested.

His eyes widened when he inhaled the smoke from the glass dick. When he exhaled, he blew the smoke out slowly from his nose and mouth simultaneously.

"Here's five thousand dollars worth of eight balls." Freedom showed B.G. the package of weighed out crack, then he added, "Do you think we can get it off?"

"With this shit, you're going to have mad people going out of space," B.G. said as his mouth twisted.

He proceeded to grab one of the weighed out packages and exited the apartment. He rounded up the neighborhood's best astronauts to take with him on his out-of-space mission. Freedom knew B.G. well, so if he gave him a free eight ball, he knew he'd come back with enough fiends *and* money to finish his entire package.

B.G. walked the streets for the next couple of days. He helped Freedom get off all of his twelve hundred grams of crack. When the duo had completed their mission, they sat and counted all of the wrinkled bills. It amounted to thirty-two thousand dollars. Freedom had a few grams left. He thought to himself, *I got enough to hit Memo off with fifteen grand.* He came back to earth when his cell phone rang. He pressed *"send"* and answered, "What's popping?"

"Yo, this Memo. Meet me on 140th and Broadway in front of Hamilton Place in an hour. It's 9 o'clock now. Be there at ten. Peace." Memo banged the phone on him.

Freedom ended the call and thought to himself, *How should I pay Memo? Should I buy another one, or should I buy five hundred grams for seventy-five hundred dollars?* He left the apartment and gave B.G. the remaining work. He told him to get rid of it and that he'd be back shortly.

He raced down the stairs with a shopping bag full of money and Freedom whistled for a taxi. He jumped in and arrived at 140th and Broadway, at Hamilton Place. He stepped out of the cab and proceeded to walk through the doors.

Inside, Memo and three other Dominican men stood around in a huddle. Memo had a pouch that contained a thousand grams of powder cocaine.

Freedom spoke. "I have twenty-two thousand dollars. I want this one and I'll pay you in three days." Freedom was ready to sell till he fell. It was on and crack-a-lacking now.

"Young Free, you passed my test. You don't have to pay me in three days. I'm giving you a week this time. So take your time," Memo stated with a smile on his face. He reached for the bag, and patted Freedom on his back.

Freedom left the building anxious as he waited for another cab to come by. He got inside of the taxi, laid back and thought, *I haven't taken a shower in three days. I haven't had any pussy either. I'll go to Mom's crib and change up.* He continued audibly this time, "Forty-second and Malcolm X Boulevard," he told the cab driver.

Chapter 4

*F*reedom arrived at his mother's building. It was where he spent most of his nights. He raced up the stairs until he reached the 11th floor. Freedom dug in his crowded pockets, pulled out his key and unlocked the door. He yelled inside, "Ma! Mommy! You here?" Without waiting for an answer, he went to his room, closed the door and began to examine the package Memo had given him. Just like before, it was fishscale coke. He placed the drugs inside of a safe in his closet, took off his clothes and jumped into the shower. He finished up and again thought to himself, *Damn, who should I call? Pam, Mercedes, or Tash?* He decided to call Mercedes. He hadn't seen Mercedes since the day he met Havoc on the train.

Mercedes, was Freedom's first real piece of ass. They both attended Rice High School located on 124th street and Lenox Avenue. Ironicly they were placed in the same home room class. One morning in their home room class, Freedom arrived ten minutes late, as usual. All of the classroom seats were taken except for a seat that sat directly beside Mercedes. Freedom flopped down in the hard wooden chair and stared at Mercedes until she felt his eyes burning into her which caused her to turn and look in his direction.

"What?" Merecedes whispered. She smiled from ear to ear,

then she shifted her weight to one side of the chair, so she could here Freedom better.

"Yo, after school, I want to holla at you." Freedom whispered. He pointed at the clock that hung on the wall above the chalk board, held up his index, middle and ring fingers, and said, "at three o'clock."

"Okay, boy." Mercedes agreed and smiled bashfully. The teacher spotted the duo, cleared her throat and said, "I hope you two don't mind if I take roll call?"

The teenagers shook their heads quickly and at the same time said, "Oh, I'm sorry."

Freedom walked around the entire school for the rest of the afternoon telling all of his homies that he and Mercedes' had a date after school.

Mercedes told all of her friends in her P.E. class, that the wildest boy in school wanted to get up with her.

Hours passed, the clock struck three, then the school bell rung. All the students exited the school building and went their separate ways. Freedom stood directly in front of the boys bathroom, noticed Mercedes from afar and yelled, "Yo, come here".

Mercedes looked, then trotted over to where Freedom waited. She looked at him, then spoke in a soft voice. "What's up boy?"

Freedom, pushed open the bathroom's door, he motioned with his head and ordered, "Follow me."

"I aint going in there with you, boy." Mercedes squenched up her face and sucked her teeth.

"Why not, nobody'll see us," Freedom assured that they wouldn't get caught.

"If I go in there with you, you better not tell anybody." Mercedes sucked her teeth, rolled her eyes, then pranced behind

Freedom.

The couple entered inside the boys bathroom.

Freedom held one of the stalls open, Mercedes entered then pulled her pants down to her knees.

Freedom pulled his pants down to his ankles, got behind her and said ,"Bend over".

When the young couple was finished, Freedom pulled his pants back up, then Mercedes pulled her tight bugs bunny panties back over her butt and said, "Promise me you won't tell anybody". Freedom placed his hands behind his back, crossed his index and middle finger and said, "I promise." They exited the bathroom and went their separate ways.

For weeks they continued to have their three o'clock meetings in the boys bathroom until Freedom's grades started to decline and he couldn't maintain his D average. He ended up dropping out of high school but he still managed to keep his secret relationship with Mercedes. When Mercedes completed high school and got a good job, they relocated their meetings to her two bed room energy efficient apartment.

Ring, ring. The phone rang twice before Mercedes answered.

"Hello," Mercedes spoke cordially into the receiver.

"What's up, Beau," Freedom asked while he put lotion on his body and brushed in his waves.

"What's up, Free? Long time no hear from," Mercedes reminded him that it had been a while since they last got up. *Literally* on his part.

"Yo, can I see you later?" Freedom asked as he continued to brush in his waves.

"What, you couldn't find another one of your ho's to fuck?" Mercedes asked. She was upset because she really loved Freedom. She just hated the fact that he ran the streets so much.

"So what, you calling yourself a ho?" Freedom laughed as

he proceeded to get dressed. He tore the tags off of his Prada suit, put it on and gazed in his full-length mirror, checking out his new outfit.

"If I'm a ho, I'm the best one you know," Mercedes smacked her lips, then added, "you can come through. I should be home around 12 o'clock." Then she ended the call.

Around 11:30 that evening Freedom left his apartment and proceeded to Mercedes' place. He arrived at her building, entered through the building's security doors, as two beautiful black women watched him from afar. As he passed, one woman stated quietly to the other "Um, damn, girl, who's that fine brother?" They stared in amazement.

Freedom stayed focused as he entered the elevator. Once inside, he pressed "8." Freedom exited onto the 8th floor, then he checked his Prada velour pants to see how they fit around his six inch white Air Force Ones. He jiggled the bottom of his pants, then continued to walk to Mercedes' apartment. He knocked on her door and waited patiently. Mercedes opened the door to her two-bedroom energy efficient apartment that she shared with her younger sister. Mercedes was in her late teens, 5'7 and 135 pounds. Her measurements were 34D-24-38. Mercedes' caramel complexion went great with her bronze hair color. She stood in front of her doorway and looked at Freedom while she loosened the belt around her blue Roberto Cavali jeans then said, "Come in." Mercedes' lips looked wet from the Chanel lip gloss she wore. She rolled her tongue then trimmed the edges of her lips in a circular motion. She continued in a sexy manner. "You know my pussy is itching for that magic stick." Mercedes reached for Freedom's hand and pulled him close.

Freedom proceeded through the door. He grabbed Mercedes by the waist with one hand and closed the door with the other. He responded. "Damn, just like I left you, hot and wet." Freedom placed his tongue on her lips and traced the shape of her mouth. He pulled her shirt above her breasts and sucked on her nipples.

Mercedes was anxious and excited. She placed her hand into Freedom's pants and caressed his rock hard wand. Mercedes knelt down on her knees, pulled Freedom's dick from his pants, inserted it into her hot and juicy mouth, then teased the head of his dick with the tip of her tongue. She peeked up at Freedom with her baby doll eyes and said, "Does that feel good?" Saliva and lip gloss dripped from the sides of her mouth as she continued. "I know you want it, put it in me." She leaned back on her sofa and pulled her pants off. Freedom pulled her panties to one side and inserted himself inside of her. He pumped in and out of her mercilessly. Mercedes dug her fingernails into his back and screamed, "Fuck me, fuck me harder!" The duo fucked for hours. When they finished, both of them sat on the living room floor and regained their composure.

Freedom looked Mercedes in the eye and said, "Mercedes, I want you to consider doing something for me." He massaged her shoulders as he continued. "I would like you and your homie, Bish, to handle some B.I. on Lenox Avenue for me." Freedom was still exhausted from what had transpired only moments ago.

"Baby, you know I haven't gotten down like that in a minute," Mercedes proclaimed. She got up and put her jeans back on. She wiggled to get them over her butt, then proceeded to the bathroom.

Freedom trotted behind her and said, "I got a feeling this could be real big. Plus, I also got an out of town mission to take care of." Freedom pulled her close and continued. "You know

I wouldn't be asking you if I didn't trust this." He gazed into her eyes.

"I know, I know." She gave Freedom a peck on the lips and smiled, then she whispered, "So when do we start?"

"Call Bish tomorrow and see if she's in. Tell her that they'll be Jimmy Choo shoes in it for her." He sounded convincing as he raised his eyebrows three quick times in a suggestive manner.

"How much work you dealing with, baby?" Mercedes questioned.

"Listen, I got work for days, so that doesn't matter. What matters is that you'll be getting money. Somewhere around eight to ten grand a day." Freedom assured his baby that everything would be safe and secure, then he continued in a fatherly manner. "I'll make sure you're in the best of hands."

Mercedes and Bish met at Rice High School. The two young ladies shared the same physical education class. The duo spent most of their hour long classes cuddled up on the bleachers exchanging boy stories.

One afternoon, the ladies were sitting on the bleachers like they normally did, not participating in any of the gym activities. Mercedes looked at her friend Bish and shouted in the lowest voice possible, "Guess what girl." Before Bish could take a shot at guessing, Mercedes continued, "Well, anyway, between me and you, I know you know that nigga Freedom. Well, we did it in the boys bathroom yesterday."

"No you didn't girl." Bish said. The look on her face was as if she had seen Jesus rise from his grave.

"Yeah, and let me tell you child, listen, that nigga got the biggest dick I've ever seen." Mercedes smiled and wobbled her head.

"That's all good, but listen to this, me and," Bish paused for a second and looked around the gym to check to see if anyone was eavesdropping. Once she decided it was safe to talk she continued. "you got to promise me you won't leak a word of this out."

Mercedes agreed. "I promise."

"Okay, well, child, me and his cousin, this nigga named Nino, fucked last night in the park, and girl, the night air was feeling good to my little ass." Bish explained. The tone is her voice told her buddy that she enjoyed herself.

"What." Mercedes sounded shocked, she placed her hand over her mouth, then she asked, "So you not with Fred anymore?"

"Yeah, but you know how that nigga is, if he finds out there will be problems." Bish said calmly with her elbows arched, then she continued, "So I hope this fool don't tell anybody."

The duo sat on the bleachers puzzled, they both looked into space and pictured what could happen if Bish's boyfriend found out that she had sex with another guy. The girls were brought back from their outta space mission when they heard the school bell ring. Mercedes jumped down from the bleachers, cupped her hands and helped Bish down.

The two teenagers exited the gym and went their separate ways. But after that conversation they felt comfortable telling each other their inner most deepest secrets and they made a vow, *Friendship over Niggas.*

Chapter 5

*M*eanwhile, out in Brooklyn ...
Havoc had put together the blueprint to the heist over in Connecticut. All week long he worked his hand with his inside source. Havoc knew the boyfriend of a housekeeper that worked for some rich doctor in Greenwich. The doctor was worth 15.5 million dollars. Since he was doing side deals on life insurance policies, he had three hundred thousand dollars in cash hidden inside of a safe. The safe was built into the wall in his master bedroom behind an early 20th century painting by Picasso. Havoc picked up is Nextel cell phone and called Rick. Rick was the boyfriend of the maid who suggested the heist.

Ring, ring. Rick's telephone buzzed.

"Hello," Rick answered.

"What's new? Everything is set, *right?* No one will be home, *correct?*" Havoc asked. He sat with one finger on his temple inside the building where he worked. He was inside the main office.

"Everything is a go. Just make sure you don't kill anyone if someone *is* home," Rick stated.

"Yo, son, I ain't trying to die either, so I hope ma fuckas ain't home," Havoc enunciated. He paused for a second and heard a beep in his phone. Then he said, "Hold on." Havoc answered the other call. "Speak to me." He stood up and paced the floor of the office. The voice on the other end sounded excited.

"Yo, everything is everything. The car is in place."

Havoc stared into space, then asked, "What kind of whip did you manage to get?"

"Big H, we got a black on black M3 BMW," the voice on the other end stated, then ended the call.

Havoc clicked back to the other line and responded. "You still there, Rick? Rick?"

Rick interrupted. "Yeah, in two days it should be all set."

"I hope so because I got babies to feed and my wife wants that new C-230 Benz." Havoc sounded demanding. He hung up the phone, closed all the blinds, locked all the doors, left the building and jumped into his large 500 SL Mercedes Benz. He picked up his Motorola car phone and proceeded to call Freedom.

Ring, ring.

"Holla at your boy," Freedom answered.

"What's popping?" Havoc asked. He laid back in the V-12 and steered with one hand.

"I've been taking care of some business," Freedom spoke with confidence. He pushed Mercedes away from kissing on his ear. He continued, "What's new?"

"I've been cooling with the wifey and kids trying to plot on this move in Connecticut. A hundred and fifty thousand dollars a piece."

"Damn, kid, that's a lot of bread. When we going to get that money?" Freedom asked.

"In two days everything should be clean and air tight. I mapped out the whole shit. Just meet me on the Metro North at 7:30 Friday night. Be there or lose out," Havoc recommended. He parked the luxury vehicle inside of his garage and proceeded to go inside his condo with his family.

Back at Mercedes' apartment, Freedom explained to her that in forty-eight hours he would have to attend to some business, then he would come and pick her up and take her on her first tour of the infamous Lenox Avenue. As he kissed her on her forehead, he said, "Make sure you talk to Bish," then he turned around to leave.

"I love you, baby," Mercedes shouted as she locked the door behind Freedom.

Freedom caught a cab back to his mother's apartment on 142nd Street and Malcolm X Boulevard. He contacted Memo. Freedom assured him that everything was going smoothly and in a few days it would be two beautiful women coming to meet him. Freedom explained that the women would have what he owed him and enough for a whole joint.

Later that night, Freedom prepared to cook the cocaine he had left from what he copped from Memo. Every time he got a new batch, he would put on his apron and become *Chef-Boy-R-Free*. He transformed one kilo into a kilo and a half. Freedom thought to himself as he finished examining his expert cooking skills, *I should see forty-five thousand dollars off of this flip. With the extra money, I can take Mercedes and Bish shopping. But tomorrow is Thursday. Damn, it's Thursday. That's not good.*

Thursdays were very dangerous in the drug world. The police department had created a special team of agents that called themselves T.N.T. because they usually targeted drug dealers and their drug spots on Tuesdays and Thursdays. Freedom stashed all of the cooked up crack and reached for his alarm clock. He set his alarm for 8 a.m. He laid his head on his pillow and fell asleep.

Hours had passed when Freedom was suddenly awakened by the buzz from the clock. He got dressed and proceeded to Mercedes' apartment. When he arrived at her building, he saw the ladies on the outside of Mercedes' apartment building. They had on hoodies and Timberland construction boots. The women had money on their minds and they dressed for the occasion. Freedom approached the couple and reached for Mercedes' hand. He asked, "What's up, Beau?" Freedom kissed the back of his friend's hand and added, "How are you doing, Bish? Long time no hear from."

Bish responded, "What's going on?" They guided Freedom to a set of steps and took a seat. Freedom explained every detail of his plan. "It takes hard work and determination to make it in this game."

He was rudely interrupted by Bish. "Look, how much money are we getting out of this deal?" Bish was still in the drug business doing her little odds and ends to pay bills.

Freedom stared at the woman and stated in a frustrated manner, "Like I was saying, we're not just trying to pay bills and buy clothes. We're trying to get out of the hood so we can fall back and breath easy."

The two beautiful teenagers looked on with their eyes wide and waited until Freedom finished his speech. Freedom began to pace back and forth. He concentrated on Bish the most. "If you want short term, I'll hit you both with five thousand dollars plus take both of y'all shopping." He hoped they opted for the long term, but with Bish being *the type to bust an "O" down with her girl, hustler,* it was uncertain what they'd do.

Mercedes and Bish both knew that if Freedom was talking about giving them five thousand dollars each, plus go on a shopping spree, then he must be talking about some serious money. So the duo agreed to be a part of Freedom's drug business. They said at the same time, "When do we start?"

"We can start in the morning and Sunday you should be ready to meet my connect for me. He'll be expecting you. So what he gives you, keep it safe, and I'll be back Monday, alright?" Freedom watched the duo to see how they felt about their new positions. Then he continued, "You should get like at least thirty thousand dollars before I come back." Freedom made sure he added a few high figures into the equation. With the idea that thirty thousand dollars could be made within only a few days, by some teenage broads at that, Bish and Mercedes would break day if they had to.

"Thirty thousand? That's a lot of cake," Bish shouted. She jumped up from her sitting position and took off her fitted hat.

"But you'll give the connect twenty-two thousand and the rest you'll put under the mattress," Freedom stated. He described the hole in the mattress so they would know exactly where to put the money. Freedom explained that his runner, B.G., would be expecting them and he would take them through step by step. Bish and Mercedes looked on like two grade school kids. When Freedom was about to leave, they shouted, "Be careful!"

Chapter 6

riday night...

It was approximately 7:25 p.m. Havoc was waiting patiently for the 7:30 train to arrive. When the train pulled up, Havoc showed his ticket and boarded the iron horse. He looked for a seat and sat uncomfortably in the cramped Metro-North locomotive. Havoc scanned the train but didn't see Freedom. Little did he know that Freedom had already boarded the train and sat two seats behind him. Freedom waited until the train started to move and reached around Havoc's neck from behind him. He whispered, "You know what it is." Freedom was fucking with Havoc, pretending to be a stickup kid.

"Damn, kid, why you didn't say anything?" Havoc was trembling but he quickly regained his composure because he couldn't let his compadre realize that he was startled. He continued, "I thought I would be on this come up alone."

Freedom plopped down in the seat beside Havoc and asked, "What's popping? Fill me in on the details."

"Yo, peep this. We'll enter the mansion through the back entrance. The safe should be in the master bedroom. It should be like three hundred thousand in there, but we have to split it with my connect," Havoc explained, as he looked at Freedom.

He then adjusted his seat all the way back for the half hour commute to Connecticut.

Freedom thought to himself about the phone conversation he and Havoc had prior and Havoc assured they would get a hundred and fifty thousand dollars to split. Suspicious, Freedom murmured, "So you and I get seventy-five g's a piece?"

"Yep, I just hope we don't have to kill anybody. It *should* go smooth, but I brought my 40 caliber just in case," Havoc explained. He peeked over at Freedom to see if he caught on to what was about to take place.

"Big homie, how we getting back to the city?" Freedom asked.

"I have this car stashed out in White Plains." Havoc assured everything would be taken care of.

Freedom watched his partner. He could sense that he was leaving something out. He asked, "So we walking to White Plains?"

Havoc quickly ended the conversation by saying, "There's our stop. Take this bag and when we get off, put those clothes on."

The duo walked through the multi-million dollar neighborhood. They both switched their outfits to the all-black clothing they had in the Louis Vuttion knapsack. They continued to walk through the maze of mansions, searching for the right address. There it stood, a big white mansion. The duo raced towards the back of the luxury establishment and noticed the entrance was open. *"Just like Rick said it would be."* The two men were amazed by the features inside of the palace. An elevator sat in the middle of the mansion and every room had marble floors. The duo finally reached the master bedroom. The painting was there, on the wall, above the king size bed. They pulled the huge picture off of the wall. Havoc began to get excited once he spotted the safe. He pulled the combination from his pocket and punched in the numbers of the combination lock. Freedom pulled on the handle. It opened. There it was—the three hundred thousand dollars, along with some jewelry. The duo grabbed the money, closed the safe and placed the Picasso painting back on the wall. They dashed back out of the huge house and raced up two blocks. There, Rick and his girlfriend sat in an old tan Buick. Freedom and Havoc jumped inside. Havoc, out of breath and excited, yelled, "We got it. We got it!"

The posse drove to I-95 South highway, got on it and headed in the direction of New York. Havoc and Rick counted out a hundred fifty thousand each.

"Yo, take this exit," Havoc shouted. He pointed out an exit that wasn't part of the plan.

"Why we taking this exit?" Rick asked. He sounded worried. He looked back at Freedom *and* Havoc.

"We need to ditch these clothes before we go back to the city." Havoc told Rick and his girlfriend that everything was going as planned. Freedom looked on. He could sense it was gonna be trouble.

"Pull over in this parking lot," Havoc sounded excited. He looked at Freedom with his eyes and with his head he motioned to Freedom to look at the getaway car. A black on black M3 BMW. The duo exited the Buick, took off their clothes and switched back into their original attire. Havoc put the old clothes *and* the money inside the trunk of the German car, but kept his gloves on. Havoc pulled the 40 caliber semi-automatic handgun from his waistline and proceeded towards Rick and his girlfriend who were waiting patiently for them to return. Havoc approached the driver's side door, pointed the barrel of his gun at the window of the Buick, opened the door and looked at Rick. With the devil in his eyes he yelled, "Give me the money, mutha fucka."

"Why are you doing this? I thought everything was all good," Rick pleaded for his life. He locked eyes with Havoc and realized that he was serious. Then he continued, "Come on, take the money, but let us go," Havoc raised his gun and let off a series of shots. The bullets penetrated through the old car, shattering the rear windows and hitting Rick and his girlfriend in their heads. The couple lay dead in a pool of blood. Havoc then reached for the money and headed over to his getaway vehicle. They got inside and jetted down I-95 South until they arrived at the Connecticut and New York border line. They paid the toll and later ditched the sports car in co-op city. The entire ride, they sat in silence.

As the duo waited for a cabi, Freedom broke the silence. "Yo, what the fuck you doing, Bee? That wasn't part of the plan. You just bodied two mutha fuckas." At first, Freedom wasn't gonna say shit. I mean two ma fuckas just lost their lives by his partner, so Free was scared shitless. He figured, "Fuck it, if the nigga was gon' blast me, I would've *been* maggot food already. Let me see what's on this nigga's mind." That's when he asked him what the fuck was up.

"Yo, did you touch anything?" Havoc asked. He knew they had on leather gloves and before Freedom could respond, Havoc continued, "No, so you good. We came off with a hundred and fifty thousand a piece."

They hopped into the taxi that had stopped to pick them up and headed into the city. Freedom glanced at his partner in crime, took a deep breath, and asked, "What else are you into?"

"Hits, heists, stocks and bonds, construction, whatever it takes to get rich. You feel me?" Havoc stated. He clutched the knapsack with the money and clothes tightly. He added, "By the way, what have you been doing all week?" He was as calm as a summer breeze.

"*Well*, I got this issue on Lenox Avenue." Freedom paused for a second then he continued. "Ten thousand dollars a night."

"Yo, kid, what you trying to get yourself, a hundred years? These crackers ain't playing no games when it comes to that tax free money. Matter of fact, circle yourself three times when we go on the next heist, I ain't trying to be no codefendant in nobody's drug case," Havoc stated. He looked at his watch and glanced over at the street sign. Havoc stated loud and clear, "Stop right here."

Havoc had made reservations at a luxury five-star hotel on 42nd Street. The duo entered the hotel, got the room key, then walked over to the elevator. Havoc pressed "15." They rode the elevator to the 15th floor and exited. They entered their suite and Freedom looked around amazed at the luxurious room. He stated, "Look, I got my situation under control. If the feds do get involved, I know how to handle them."

"Yo, son, I've been hustling since the early 90's when niggas were getting hit with twenty and thirty years. Them niggas is still laying on their racks." Havoc dumped all the money onto the table and continued. "Now-a-days, ma fuckas can't hold water. I got a better way."

The duo counted out a hundred fifty thousand dollars a piece, gave each other their customary handshake that ended with a snap, and Freedom proceed to go to Malcolm X Boulevard to count out his money and calm his nerves.

Chapter 7

*B*ack on Lenox Avenue...
Mercedes and Bish sat in B.G.'s small studio apartment and served every fiend that B.G. brought by. The duo knew that on Sunday morning, Memo would be waiting for them in front of Hamilton Place. In the meantime, they gathered up as much money as they could.

"I never seen this much money before. Freedom must be into something heavy," Bish stated as she counted the wrinkled money. Bish reached inside of her bra and pulled out a sack of marijuana that she had been saving for a special event. The duo stared at each other in amazement.

"Yo, bitch, we don't have no cigars," Mercedes smacked her lips. She looked around the entire apartment in search of a Dutch Master cigar. With no luck, she placed her hand on her hip and suggested, "Let's go to the store." The ladies stashed the money and cocaine and proceeded to the store.

The Bodega on 139th Street and Lenox Avenue was the only store in the vicinity that sold vanilla flavored Dutch Masters. When they got to the store, Mercedes went inside to purchase the cigars because she looked older than Bish. Bish remained outside where she spotted a nice looking dude, tall, in his early

20's, about 185 pounds, looking her way. He was on the other side of the street. He ran across the street and asked, "Yo, Boo, what you doing around here?" The stranger was sizing Bish up, admiring her whole package.

"You talking to me?" Bish looked shocked as she pointed to herself.

The guy approached her and with his hand on his head said, "I must've died and gone to heaven." He looked her up and down then continued. "Hi, my name is Trey. This is my hood and I've never seen you around here before."

Before Bish could answer, Mercedes came out of the store and said, "Are you ready?" She fixed the strings on her Timberland boots.

"Damn, it's *two* of y'all," Trey remarked as he looked over the duo. He reached for Mercedes' hand to greet her. "My name is Trey," he introduced himself once again.

Before he could finish, Bish said in a sarcastic tone of voice, "He's the man over here and this is *his* hood." The ladies laughed and walked back towards B.G.'s crack house. They waved goodbye to Trey and kept it moving.

"Nice to meet y'all fine young ladies. Maybe next time you're in town we can kick it," Trey yelled through the palm of both of his hands.

Trey was the boss on 139th Street and Lenox. If a nickel bag was sold in the park, he had in on it. He stood at the corner looking puzzled as he watched the duo walk back up the street. He waited until they disappeared and then dashed back into the projects.

Bish and Mercedes arrived back at the crack spot. Mercedes turned and looked at Bish and stated, "He *was* fine. You should've gotten his number." She rolled her eyes.

"He'll be around," Bish said. She dumped the tobacco out

of the cigar onto the table and lined the sack of marijuana inside of it. She rolled the blunt of weed tight, then licked both sides of the blunt to make sure nothing fell out of the ends. She lit the Dutch Master, inhaled the weed slowly, blew smoke through her nose, and coughed. "This is the bomb as dro, bitch. By the way, when Free coming back?"

"He said he's going to call me," Mercedes said, then grabbed the heavily packed cigar.

B.G. continued to run sales all throughout the night. He sold the last ounce of crack to Mike. Mike and B.G. used to be partners back in the day, but they both fell victim to their own supply. B.G. and Mike beamed up to Scotty for the remainder of the night. Mercedes and Bish had fallen asleep early. They were tired from the constant knocking at the door, serving fiends all weekend. Mercedes was then awakened from the vibration of her cell phone.

"Hello. Hello," Mercedes answered. She jumped up to see if the money was still in place. Mercedes checked the dough while Freedom spoke.

"Yo, what's up, Boo? I'm calling you to make sure you're ah-ight." Freedom sounded energized.

"Everything went smooth. We're finished," Mercedes stretched.

"Memo should be waiting for you and Bish. You guys got fifteen minutes," Freedom explained as his cell phone began breaking up with static. "I'll see you later, ah-ight?" then he ended the call.

"Bish, get up, get up," Mercedes yanked and pulled on Bish's arm. Once up, the duo grabbed the money, placed it inside of a pouch, exited the apartment building and waited for a cab. They got inside the cab and headed toward Broadway. They reached 140th Street and Broadway in five minutes. They exited the taxi and walked up into the building. Memo stood inside of the building's hallway and directed the ladies inside of an apartment he used for transactions. Memo greeted the ladies. "I'm Memo and you guys are late." He closed the door behind them and locked it.

"Late?" Bish questioned. She looked down at her watch and continued, "We're only ten minutes late. Do you have the package?" She wiggled her neck and placed her hand on her tiny waist.

"Easy, easy. I was only kidding. It's right here in this bag," Memo laughed. He handed Bish the shopping bag then said, "Tell Free to get at me next week."

The ladies then proceeded back outside and waited for the next cabi to come by. Mercedes and Bish had the cocaine in their possession. They were scared and nervous. A taxi stopped and the chicks climbed inside, trembling as they sat low inside the rear of the vehicle. They stared at each other until they arrived at their destination. Once out of the livery cab, Mercedes reached for her phone and called Freedom.

Ring, ring.

"Speak to me," Freedom answered.

"We got it. Mission is complete," Mercedes whispered.

"Good. I'll get at you later. Sit tight and tell B.G. not to worry, that I got him when I get there," Freedom assured, then hung up the call. The duo raced up the stairs, stashed the cocaine and waited patiently for Freedom.

Chapter 8

Freedom arrived at his mother's house and raced up the stairs to his room. He put the hundred and fifty thousand in his safe with the rest of his money he had earned from the heist and his drug dealing. He thought to himself, *I now got two hundred thousand plus more work.* Freedom was startled when he heard his mother's voice. He headed down the stairs to greet his mom, who was a recovering crack fiend. For five years, she'd been sober.

If you would have seen her five years prior, she resembled a light skinned Whitney Houston.Freedom's mom would walk the streets late at night, chasing the feeling she got from her first time smoking crack cocaine.

Unfortunely, after every bag she purchased, she was unable to catch that same high. One late night Freedom's mother strolled around the neighborhood in search of her daily fix, until she came across a slim young cat in his late teens. Freedom's mom approached the teenager. Her mouth twisted as she spoke softly, "Where can I get some work?"

The young man gazed at Freedom's mom, then asked.

"What you looking for?"

"A dub." Freedom's mom said, her lips were chapped and ashy.

"Hold up, for a minute." The teen assured that he would be right back, then he dashed in hot pursuit to his stash spot. He pulled out a plastic bag from underneath a rock that contained forty capsules with blue and red tops. The young teenager dipped back from behind the project building, approached Freedom's mom, held his hand out with 10 blue top capsules, then continued. "Choose which one you want."

Freedom's mom eyes widened, she looked amazed. She fumbled through each crack vile and decided on the fattest one. She dug inside of her bra, pulled a wrinkled 20 dollar bill out, handed it to the boy and murmured, "If its good, I'll be back."

"I'll see you later because my shit is the bomb diggedy."

The young man lied. He watched Freedom's mom's fragile body prance back up the street. She entered the basement door of her building then pulled out her favorite crack pipe that she had made from a miniature plastic container that had a rose inside of it that she had purchased a couple of days prior. She threw the rose away and kept the bottle for her outta space trips.

Freedom's mom placed the hard substance on the tip of the container and flicked her Bic lighter that she had hyped up so that the flame extended real high. She tilted the lighter, placed the flame directly on the substance, placed her lips around the other end of the container, then she inhaled. She held the smoke in until she counted to five. She exhaled, coughed, then called Earl.

She whispered to herself, "Damm, that little ma'fucka got me ." She called Earl again, looked into the sky and continued, "He sold me some beat."

From that night on she'd been clean. Freedom's mom promised herself that she wouldn't smoke crack cocaine ever again. For five years she's maintained her factory job and made ends meet so her baby boy could have a roof over his head.

"Do you have a few dollars so I can go to the supermarket?" Freedom's mother asked as she gave him a tight bear hug and a kiss on the cheek.

"How much do you need?" Freedom asked reaching inside of his pockets and pulling out a crisp hundred dollar bill.

His mother grabbed the bill. "Thank you, baby. I'll be back to cook something," Freedom's mother stated. She turned and walked out of the apartment smiling.

Freedom thought to himself, *I got a lot of work to do tomorrow. Maybe I'll take the girls shopping.* He snapped out of his thought when his cell phone chirped.

"What's hood?" he answered.

"It's Pam, Boo. I got a plug on something you might be interested in. Some brand new B.M.W.s. All of them are off of the showroom floor. They're going for fifty grand a pop," Pam said in a professional manner.

Pam was an old friend of Freedom's. She spent most of her time running scams on the Internet. Every month she would get cell phones and turn them on for people illegally. She would then sell them for a small fee.

"Yo! Pam, get at me tomorrow around eightish. We'll meet in the village on 6th Avenue," Freedom stated. He hung up the call and thought to himself, *This could separate me from those "in the way dudes." I can now cop me my first real car.*

Freedom went back upstairs to his room. He was exhausted from the heist so he dosed off to sleep. He was later awakened by the chirp of his cell phone. After fumbling around for a second in his bed, he found it and answered, "What's up?"

"Oh, no, don't tell me your ass is still asleep. It's 7:45 in the ma fucking morning," Pam yelled angrily.

"Yo! I'll be over there in a second," Freedom said. He hung up the call, jumped up, took a shower, and began to get dressed. He looked at his large collection of fitted hats and finally found a black on black New York Yankees fitted to go with his three hundred and fifty dollar *E. Visu* jeans. He caught a cab, hopped in and when he pulled up to 6th Avenue, his face lit up when he saw Pam inside of a crisp blue, candy painted 745i B.M.W. He exited the cab and dashed across the busy street. He took off his hat and said, "Damn, baby, this car looks better than you." He smiled.

Pam was a real knockout though. She was dark brown skinned, around 5'7, 135 pounds. Her measurements were 36DD-26-42. She stepped out of the vehicle with some *Jimmy Choo* sandals and a *Chanel* sundress that clenched her thighs and butt. She walked around to the passenger side of the sports car and motioned for Freedom to get in the driver's seat. Then she said, "I told you I wasn't bullshitting."

Freedom climbed into the oversized B.M.W. as Pam continued. "Do you like it and did you bring the money?" She had a charming smile and it was currently on overdrive.

"Of course I love it, but I didn't bring the money with me. We have to go back to my rest and get it." Freedom explained.

"That's cool. You need to test drive this joint anyway." She handed Freedom the key then continued, "I hope you have your license." She maintained her smile.

Freedom moved his chair all the way back. Then he leaned the seat back until he could just barely see over the steering wheel. With one hand he put the foreign car in drive, gave Pam a smile, then drove off.

"I told you I'll get shit popping off. Next month, I'll have some Benzos, same price," Pam said as she showed Freedom how the navigational system worked.

They arrived at Freedom's apartment building in no time. Freedom jumped out of the car and raced upstairs. Before he entered his building, he looked back at the 745i one more time, smiled, then proceeded through the security doors. A few moments later, he came back out with a plastic bag containing fifty thousand dollars. He reentered the car, handed Pam the money and as Pam checked the funds, he said, "I'll wait with you until the cab comes. To make sure nothing doesn't pop off, na mean." Free winked at Pam.

She looked Freedom up and down and gently bit her bottom lip. She said, "Call me sometime so I can give you some of this hot, wet pussy down here," Pam grabbed Freedom's hand and placed it in between her legs.

Freedom murmured, "Maybe I'll take you up on that offer one day." He glanced at her and smiled.

"I hope it can be tonight," Pam offered. She forced one of Freedom's fingers inside of her to show him how wet she was.

"Damn, baby, I'll get at you at 10 o'clock. Don't stand me up," Freedom grunted. He smelled his index finger, then he inserted it into his mouth, tasting Pam's juices.

"You just make sure you tell them other bitches that you have plans," Pam stated. She glanced down the street and spotted a cab.

"Don't worry about that. I need some of that good shit you got in my life," Freedom assured Pam. He kissed her on both cheeks, then opened the door to the cab for her.

"Don't be late," Pam said. She blew him a kiss as the cab drove off.

Chapter 9

hen Freedom arrived at B.G.'s apartment, he picked up his Motorola car phone and called Mercedes.

Ring! Ring!

"Hello," she answered.

"What's up? Everything is good, right?" Freedom cut the car off and laid back into the leather seats.

"Yes, baby, everything is fine. When are you coming through? I'm tired of sitting around here," Mercedes sounded frustrated.

"Well, bring the money you have left over downstairs. I'm outside. It's time to go shopping," Freedom stated in a pimply manner.

"Shopping?" Mercedes screamed. She hung up the phone, told Bish to come on, grabbed the rest of the money and headed outside.

When the duo got outside, their mouths dropped and their eyes widened in amazement. Bish questioned, "Is this yours?" She couldn't wipe the smile off her face if it was drawn on a chalkboard.

"Come on, baby, I stunt, but I don't front, of course, it's mines." He unlocked all of the doors with the remote from his key. The ladies jumped inside and Bish stared at Freedom as if to say that she wanted to sex him up right there on the spot. Bish passed Freedom the bag of money and grabbed his hand to show him she was feeling him. She winked her eye at Freedom so that Mercedes wouldn't notice it. The threesome then headed for Madison Avenue. They spent the day window shopping and purchasing all the latest designer clothing and shoes. When the trio was finished, they loaded up the luxury sedan with all of their shopping bags. Freedom smiled at Mercedes and asked, "Did you guys have any problems?"

Before Mercedes could answer, Bish interrupted. "Yeah, it was this one dude from the projects on 139th Street and Lenox Avenue. He kept asking us who we were."

"Oh, that's the enemy. He's probably mad because I'm taking all of his customers," Freedom explained. He adjusted his eight-disc C.D. changer as he continued. "He's been over there for a minute, but no need to worry. By the way, where are you ladies going?" Freedom looked at Bish through the rearview mirror, then brought his attention over to Mercedes who was riding shotgun in the front passenger seat.

"To my crib out on Long Island," Bish answered.

"I'll pick you guys back up on Friday so we can do the same things, ah-ight?" Freedom stated as he played with Mercedes' pubic hairs. He put two of his fingers inside of her while she lay back and moaned.

"Damn, baby, I want to fuck," Mercedes said as she humped Freedom's hand.

Freedom quickly changed the subject. He knew he hadn't been with Mercedes in about a week. He pulled his fingers out of her and wiped them off on her thigh. The trio arrived at Bish's parents' house. Freedom asked, "Damn, Bish, why you be in the city so much when you got a crib like this?" He stared at the mini mansion.

"Maybe one day I can show you around," Bish said in a sexy tone of voice. The duo grabbed their shopping bags out from the crowded trunk.

Mercedes looked on and sensed the vibe between Bish and Freedom. She intervened. "Excuse me, you two can cut all that bullshit out. You're my piece of dick, so what's up for tonight anyway?" she rolled her eyes at Bish then placed her arms around Freedom's waist.

"I told you I got business to attend to," Freedom stated.

"I'll remember this when you want some ass," Mercedes said. She poked her lip out and added, "At least give me a kiss."

Freedom kissed her and said, "Yo! I'll holla at you later, Bish." The girls gathered their bags and headed for the huge house. Freedom waited for the chicks to reach the door before he pulled off.

"Damn, Mercedes, that ma fucka must be getting crazy money," Bish stated as the two pranced up the driveway.

"Yeah, he told me he was in some heavy shit. I hope he buys us a C-230 Benz," Mercedes chuckled.

When the duo reached the door, they turned around and blew Freedom goodbye kisses to assure him that they were okay.

Freedom pulled off. He made it back to the city in no time, picked up his cell phone and gave Havoc a call as he painted the town.

Ring. Ring.

"What's going on?" Havoc answered.

"What's good, Kikko?" Freedom asked, as he lay back into the comfortable leather seats of his whip.

"I'm cooling, playing with my wife and kids," Havoc said proudly.

"Damn, kid, you live a boring ass life," Freedom stated, as he was getting closer to his apartment building.

"That's the only way to keep them boys off of you. So what's popping?" Havoc asked.

"I was letting you know a nigga coped a quarter to eight," Freedom stated proudly.

"Okay, little homie, you're in the big leagues now, but listen, stay low until you see those m's, then you blow, you feel me?" Havoc said in a fatherly manner. He continued, "Don't be pushing that shit on 1-4-2 either. That's all you need is for the police to be catching feelings and shit."

"Yo, I'm good. Just get at me when that other jump off goes through," Freedom said.

"I'll get at you, but remember, stay low key until you get some clean money, you feel me?" Havoc reiterated before hanging up the phone. He looked at his baby boy, then thought to himself, *This is gonna be the last heist. Then I can finally build my own construction company and get this temp agency for my wife to run.*

Chapter 10

*F*reedom was nearing his building when his cell phone chirped. Ring. Ring.

"What's up? Speak to me," Freedom answered as he searched for a parking spot.

"What's up, baby? You still coming through or what?" asked Pam. She was at home thinking about all of the shit she was gonna do once she got Freedom under the covers.

"Sure, why wouldn't I be?" Freedom sounded excited. His eyes opened wide when he saw a car leaving from a parking place. He continued, "I'll be around there about tenish."

"Okay. I live in building 325 on Tremont Avenue. My apartment number is 5. I'll buzz you in," Pam gave Freedom directions to her pad. Then she hung up with the call.

Freedom raced up the stairs of his building to put the shopping bags up. He noticed that B.G. had called his house phone. He picked up his cell and returned the call.

Ring! Ring! Ring! Ring!

"What's up?" B.G. answered.

"What's popping? You took forever to answer the phone. Is everything alright?" Freedom questioned. He picked his car keys up and proceeded to exit his crib once again.

"Yo, kid, that nigga, Trey, been asking mad questions. He told me to tell you that he don't want to see you back in this area *or* any of your bitches. He said he'll murder you if you don't comply," B.G. explained. He was afraid for his boss' life.

"Yo, don't worry about nothing. I'll take care of it. In the morning, I'll be through there," Freedom stated. He backed out of his cramped parking space, hung up his cell and headed for Pam's crib.

Freedom drove down Tremont Avenue searching for Pam's address until he saw building 325. He continued up the avenue about fifty yards, parked and walked to Pam's building. Once inside the apartment building, he buzzed the speaker to apartment 5 and Pam rang him in, where she met him at her door. Freedom entered the classy pad, looked Pam up and down, grabbed her arm and spun her around so he could admire what she had on. Pam wore a red see-through Victoria Secret lingerie outfit. Freedom wiped the sweat from his brow and said, "Damn, baby, don't do it to me like that. You gonna make me have a heart attack." He playfully placed his hand on the side of his chest where his heart was located.

"Can you handle it?" Pam asked as she passed Freedom a wine glass full of champagne.

"*Can I handle you?*" Freedom asked. He pulled Pam close, kissed her, then removed his clothes. He took Pam's tight fitting lingerie off, then kissed her entire body. He squatted down and placed his tongue on Pam's clit, nibbling on it as he held her open with two of his fingers. Once his fingers and face were covered with Pam's juices, Freedom stood up with a dick as hard as a geometry test. He backed Pam against the wall of her living room and demanded that she turn around. "Turn your ass around!"

Pam turned around and poked her fat ass out with juice

dripping down her leg. Freedom gripped her hips and pumped in and out of her. Her moans got louder and louder with each stroke.

"I'm cumming, I'm cumming," she screamed within the first minute.

"Cum all over me baby," Freedom stated excitedly as he rode her like he owned her.

The two lovebirds finished up and laughed in enjoyment. Pam said, "You go, boy!" she sat with her legs crossed then she added, "You know that's *my* dick now," she pulled Freedom close by his penis and looked seductively at him.

"You know my shit is the bomb," Freedom proudly stated. He added, "But I can't wait to bite that pussy again."

Freedom opened Pam's thick brown thighs and gently caressed her clit with the tip of his tongue until his tongue was numb. The two made love all night and all through the morning. Freedom dozed off for a few hours, but was awakened by the vibration of his cell phone.

Ring! Ring!

"Speak to me," Freedom answered with a crackle in his voice.

"Yo! It's B.G. I seen Trey last night again. He said he knows I'm running you sales and if you didn't bounce from the area, he was going to kill you," B.G. stated.

"This nigga must not know who I am. Yo, if you see that clown again, tell him I said suck my dick." Freedom assured B.G. that he had everything under control.

Freedom put his clothes back on and thought to himself, *This dude must've heard that I was on 142nd. But now he's playing with my money. I can't let this nigga run me off the block.*

Freedom continued to think to himself with his fist on the tip of his nose and mouth until he was startled by Pam.

"What's wrong, baby?" Pam asked, as she massaged his shoulders.

Freedom picked up his cell phone and dialed Havoc's number

Ring! Ring!

"What's good, playboy?" Havoc answered. He noticed Freedom's number.

"Yo, I got a small problem and I might need your help," Freedom said. He got up, kissed Pam's forehead, got dressed then left her apartment.

"It's 8 o'clock in the morning. What could possibly be your problem?" Havoc asked. He looked at his watch again and sighed.

"This kid is trying to cut in on my chips. He said if I don't leave the block that he'd kill me," Freedom explained. He jumped inside of his car and tucked himself low in the driver's seat.

"Yo! How much money you think this kid is worth?" Havoc asked in a curious tone. "I hope he's worth some millions if he's talking about killing ma fuckas." He chuckled to himself. It seemed like everything that came to his mind had to be about money.

"He's probably worth a couple hundred thousands," Freedom answered. He sat and rolled a blunt of purple haze weed.

"*Only a few hundred thousand* and he's running shit over there?" Havoc laughed. He said, "Well, meet me on 1-2-5th and 7th Avenue. I'll be in a platinum colored S500 Benz around 10 o'clock. Peace." He hung up the call.

Havoc later came driving up 125th Street and spotted Freedom standing on the outside of his B.M.W. Havoc pulled over and motioned for Freedom to get in his car. Freedom got in, gave Havoc their customary handshake and stated, "Damn, son, you doing it real big." He looked Freedom over noticing the new gear and the jewels. Then he looked over at Freedom's seven series B.M.W. "Let's go collect this little paper homie," Havoc said. He showed Freedom his 40 caliber semi-automatic handgun.

"Damn, son, it's too early for that," Freedom said hesitantly. He looked his partner in the eye to see if he was serious.

"That's when he'll least expect it. You said you had a problem, right? Well, let's go solve that ma fucka then," Havoc said in a bossy tone.

The duo headed over to 139th Street and Lenox Avenue where Trey usually hung out. In front of a bodega on the corner, Freedom spotted Trey and motioned with his head.

"There he is right there," Freedom said. He hesitated because he wasn't sure what his friend would do. Havoc drove the big body Mercedes Benz right up to where Trey was standing with a couple of female friends.

Freedom was trembling. He rolled down his window and said, "Yo, what's the deal, Trey?" Freedom was tucked low with his hat pulled down low to his eyes.

Trey didn't recognize who Freedom was. He walked up to the car. He thought it was a customer looking for some weight. Trey approached the car and realized it was Freedom.

"You wanted to see me, right?" Freedom asked as he got out of the car. Havoc exited the vehicle as well.

Trey realized that he was outnumbered. He looked both ways to see if his posse was near, but saw no sign of them. Trey stated, "Yo, kid, I've been over here from day one and you're trying to come over here and lock down my turf. It's not going to happen," Trey sounded confident. He crossed his arms and glared at both Freedom and Havoc. The ladies were still hanging around and Trey had to prove to them that he wasn't pussy.

"Yo, son, we're not trying to make any deals. Your time is up," Havoc said sternly. He gave Freedom the key to the car. Havoc signaled to his partner to drive as he forced Trey into the back seat of the Mercedes *with* the help of his semi automatic.

Trey pleaded. "I ain't trying to die. I just wanted some ends. I'm doing bad. Look kid, you can continue doing you." He looked at Havoc who had a nice grip on him and his gun pointed at Trey's liver. Once the broads saw the heat, they broke north.

"Yo, all you had to do was step aside, and it wouldn't have come to this," Freedom explained, as he followed directions from Havoc.

"Yo, turn down here into this scrap yard. I do a lot of work over here," murmured Havoc. He continued in a serious tone. "Where do you live? I just might spare you if you tell me," he nudged Trey with the nose of the gun.

"I live next to the Deegan, near Yankee Stadium," Trey answered. He looked on nervously as his body shook.

Freedom pulled the 500 into the yard and found a spot to park away from the entrance.

"Get out," Havoc yelled and cocked his gun.

The trio stood in front of the car. Trey dropped to his knees. He pleaded again for his life. "Please, don't kill me. Freedom, don't let him do this to me." He looked at Freedom, then over at Havoc. Havoc noticed the tears in Trey's eyes, but he didn't give a fuck. Dude was talking some gangsta shit and now that the drop was on *him*, his bitch ass wanna cry. Fuck that.

Havoc pulled the trigger, unloading the entire clip into Trey's body. Blood was all over the place. Havoc then searched the corpse for Trey's keys and found them along with his wallet in his pants pocket. The duo jumped back into the huge sedan and raced to Trey's apartment up in the Bronx. They ransacked his small studio apartment until Freedom found something. "I got it," He held up a Tide box containing a hundred and fifty thousand of Trey's hard earned drug money.

The duo left the apartment and Havoc walked past the 500 waving to his homie to follow him.

"Yo, where you going? You leaving your car?" Freedom asked. He looked confused as he walked down the avenue with Havoc.

"Come on, kid, you should know me by now. I would've never, ever drove my shit to hot ass Harlem to do that shit," Havoc explained, as he whistled for a taxi. He continued, "That car was taken from some kid that owes me money out in Brooklyn."

"So what you want me to do with the money?" Freedom asked. He showed Havoc the box of Tide with the money in it.

"Yo, go to your crib, count it out and we'll meet later when it gets dark," Havoc said, getting into a yellow cab. He also added, "Yo, leave those drugs alone." He winked at Freedom and hopped in the back seat.

Freedom caught the train back to Harlem and thought to himself, *I just seen three people get murdered in less than two weeks. This can't be happening to me.*

Chapter 11

Fifteen minutes later...
Freedom got off the train on 125th and Broadway. He walked down the block to 7th Avenue, jumped inside of his car and lit his blunt. Freedom checked his voice mail on his cell phone and listened to a few messages from B.G., Bish and Mercedes. One message interested him, the message from Bish.

"What's up, nigga? Mercedes went home, so if you come through, I can give you a tour of my parents' crib. Give me a call back A.S.A.P."

Freedom thought to himself. *Damn, this bitch is crazy, but she is fine as hell, and my cousin said she had some good pussy.* Freedom snapped out of his thought. He took long slow pulls off his marijuana blunt. He reached his apartment building and raced up the stairs to his room. He closed his door, opened his safe, and placed the hundred and fifty thousand dollars inside of it. He stared into space and thought, *Well, I don't have to worry about Trey anymore. I can go out there tomorrow and act as if nothing ever happened. Let me call this chicken to see what's up with her.*

Ring! Ring!

"Hello," Bish answered.

"What's going on?" Freedom asked as he lay back on his

bed and adjusted his pillow under his neck. "Where's Mercedes?" he asked cautiously.

"I know you got my message, so don't call here looking for Mercedes," Bish yelled through the phone.

"What do you mean?" Freedom smiled, as he played with his pubic hair. "That's my wifey."

"Don't play games. I know you want me. I knew that when I used to mess around with your crazy ass cousin," Bish stated with confidence.

"Yeah, you have put on a little weight since then, plus he did tell me you had the best pussy in the city," Freedom said, as he covered the receiver to block his laughter.

"So when you coming over?" she asked. Bish was smiling from ear to ear on the other end of the phone.

"Yo, I'm not trying to mess up my relationship with Mercedes *at all*, plus, we're handling business. I'm definitely not trying to fuck *that* up," Freedom pointed out.

"I ain't either. I love money and I'm not the one to kiss and tell," Bish assured. She had Freedom on the line, the bait had been caught, now her trifling ass just needed to reel him in.

"So, I'll keep that in mind, and I'll get at *you*. I got your number now, so keep that shit tight," Freedom said. Then he hung up the phone and dozed off.

The next day, Freedom had awakened and caught a taxi over to B.G.'s apartment. He noticed that they had flowers up on the corner of 139th Street to remember Trey. When he hit 142nd Street, Freedom got out of the cab and dashed inside of his crack spot. B.G. had the door already opened. He noticed Freedom from the window. They gave each other a hug, and Freedom handed B.G. a small package of crack.

"Damn, kid, I needed this eye opener. The streets are bare

right now. You know what happened to Trey, right?" B.G. shook as he took a long pull on his glass pipe. When he blew the smoke out, his eyes closed in relief. He said, "Some kids from Brooklyn kidnapped Trey the other day and these nuts left their car at his crib."

"Word?" Freedom asked. He acted like he was shocked. Then added, "I seen the flowers, so I knew something happened."

"Yeah, the talk around town is the nigga owed them niggas money," B.G. stated. He took another hit and continued. "It hasn't been shit *this* good on the block since the last time you was here."

"Yo, I'm about to whip up some *come back*. Tell your friends, the hard white is back," Freedom said. He got up, grabbed a pot and began dumping the cocaine inside of it. He added the baking soda to it and got it popping.

As the time flew by, B.G. rounded up fiends throughout the entire neighborhood. Freedom continued to prepare his special dish while the fiends waited in line like they were waiting on welfare cheese. When Freedom was done cooking, he sold half of his package on the spot. When things slowed down, he sat down and rolled up a cigar full of marijuana and called Bish.

Ring! Ring!

"Hello," she answered.

"What's popping?" Freedom asked, as he lit his blunt. He licked the tip of his finger so he could make sure the Dutch Master burned correctly.

Her smile appeared again. "I thought you was full of some bullshit. So are you coming through or what?" Bish asked in a sexy manner. She couldn't wait to fuck Freedom. After Mercedes and Freedom would get together, Mercedes would always end up telling her friend how good Freedom was at eating pussy *and* laying the pipe.

"Yo, it's 2 o'clock in the ma fucking morning. If I come all the way out to Long Island, you better be ready to give me some pussy," Freedom barked. He took slow pulls on his blunt.

"Yo! I'm going to be in a T-shirt and panties, so hurry up," Bish said, then hung up the phone.

Freedom looked at the phone, then the blunt, and left B.G.'s crack spot. He caught a cab to his car on Malcolm X Boulevard. Then he proceeded out to Long Island.

An hour later, he was outside of Bish's house. He exited his car and walked up to the door. He knocked, but before he could continue to knock, Bish opened the door. She stood 5'4", around 120 pounds, and had on a black T-shirt that said, *My boyfriend is gone out of town*. She also had on some black leather Baby Phat thongs. She let Freedom enter the crib, closed the door, then guided him up the stairs to her bedroom. Once inside the bedroom, she said very spicy like, "Let me show you what you've been missing." She smiled and started peeling.

"You don't have any cameras around and shit, do you?" Freedom asked in a sarcastic tone. He looked Bish up and down and grabbed her small frame.

"I like it rough. Choke me and pull my hair. Then throw me on the bed," Bish stated as she grabbed Freedom's hand and placed it up to her throat. With her other hand, she pulled her panties to the side and lay back on the bed.

"Damn, girl, you are freaky," Freedom said with one eyebrow raised.

"Come on, take those clothes off," Bish replied, helping Freedom remove his clothes. She pulled his dick out and played with the tip of it. She told him to put it in her butt. The more he spanked and pumped Bish's asshole, the more her moans got louder. She gripped the mattress and bit the pillow until Freedom came all over her back.

After she recuperated, she said, "I told you my shit was good." Then she flopped back down on the bed.

"Yeah, my nigga was right, you do got it going on," Freedom assured Bish that she handled her business.

"Are you spending the night?" Bish asked, then started caressing Freedom's chest.

"Yo, you better not ever tell Mercedes what happened," Freedom stated. Then he grabbed Bish's waist and cuddled up with her.

Freedom was later awakened when Bish pulled and tugged on his hard prick with her lips and mouth. He noticed that his cell vibrated.

Ring! Ring!

"What's good?" Freedom answered. He gripped the back of Bish's head allowing her to take long slow strokes in with her mouth.

"Where are you?" Mercedes asked in an excited tone.

"I'm taking care of some business," Freedom replied. He put the cover over Bish's head so Mercedes couldn't hear Bish's moans.

"Are we getting up or what?" she asked. Mercedes hadn't seen Freedom in a minute. Every time it was time to chill, Freedom either had to do something or her and Bish were in the spot working like immigrants in a sweatshop.

"Baby, I'll get at you later. We'll spend the entire day together," Freedom assured Mercedes. A second later, he gushed a load into Bish's mouth. Then he slowly hung up the phone.

Freedom got up, took a shower, and thought to himself, *Damn, what did I do. I hope this chick can hold water and not tell Mercedes what happened.* Freedom put his clothes back on and answered his once again ringing cell phone.

Ring! Ring!

"What's hood?" Freedom answered as he walked down the staircase.

"What's popping, kid? What's good for tonight? Because I got this kid who wants a half a joint, you good?" Nino asked. Nino was Freedom's cousin.

"Of course, tell them it's ten-five," Freedom informed him. He left Bish's crib and headed for Nino's hideout. He told him he'd be there in a half hour.

Chapter 12

Freedom arrived in front of his cousin's building. Nino, Freedom's cousin on his father's side of the family, was three years older than Freedom. Nino had been home for two years now after doing five years for attempted murder. He had stabbed Bish's ex-boyfriend in self defense. Bish's ex had accused the two of sleeping together for the past two years. Nino had been living an honest lifestyle. Had been working, going to college and making a few ends meet by introducing Freedom to customers that he knew.

One night, Nino and Bish got together like they normally did so they could make out in the park. The two secret love birds were unaware that they had been followed by Bish's boyfriend. Nino laid the blanket on the ground underneath the monkey bars as usual. He looked at Bish with his big brown eyes then asked. "Are you ready to make daddy happy?"

"Yes." Bish smiled as she nodded her head. She positioned herself on the blanket, pulled her tight fitted skirt up to her hips, then she laid back and spread her legs apart. "What you waiting for?" She asked Nino seductively.

"Damn, girl, you know you got the best pussy in the city." Nino assured. He pulled his pants down to his knees, got on top of Bish in the famous missionary position, gently inserted himself inside of her and uttered, "Um, Um this shit is the bomb."

"Fuck me, fuck me, daddy." Bish moaned with tears in her eyes. She bit Nino's neck then pulled him close. She whispered, "My boyfriend's thing is so little, he can't work the middle like you."

"Yo, don't even mention him right now." Nino smiled.

He pumped in and out of Bish's hot, wet box. With every stroke he took, he peeked down at his penis and admired how wet Bish was.

Then all of a sudden Bish's boyfriend jumped out of the bushes with a swiss army knife in hand. He looked at the duo and stated with anger in his voice, "I knew it, I knew it."

"Wait a minute, please don't bug out, let me explain, its not what you think baby." Bish tried to brush up on her psychology skills.

"Fuck you and this nigga." Bish's boy friend cried. He swung the 5 inch knife at Nino's head and throat. Nino ducked and dodged until he was able to wrap his arms around Bish's boyfriend's neck.

Nino put him in the sleeper choke hold. Bish's boyfriend, dazed from the pressure around his adam's apple, dropped the weapon then Nino quickly picked it up and began stabbing the dude in the chest. Bish's boyfriend fell to the ground. Nino stood over top of him and repeatedly stabbed him.

Bish, with tears in her eyes, grabbed Nino and yelled, "Stop, stop, don't kill him."

Nino looked at Bish with the devil in his eye, turned, gazed back at his victim then enunciated, "You're a lucky ma' fucka, because if this bitch didn't love you I'd kill your ass."

Nino dashed out of the park. He stayed on the low for

weeks after the brutal incident until his name started ringing bells. He decided to turn himself in due to a lack of funds. Nino was unable to post his $500,000 bond. He sat in jail until he was convinced by his attorney that if he took the attempted murder to trial he would see thirty years because his finger prints *and* the victim would burn him in court. So Nino decided to sign the five year plea deal. He was later shipped up north. There, he attended school, and completed the G.E.D program. He also earned a few college credits. On the day of his release he vowed that he would never, ever, get involved with another married woman, especially Bish.

"Damn, kid, this you?" Nino asked. He walked up to Freedom's car and as he was admiring the 20 inch wheels, he said, "Come in, the dude is inside."

"Ah-ight." He retrieved the cocaine from out of his stash spot and followed Nino into the apartment building.

"Yo, this is Stretch, and Stretch, this is Free, my cousin," Nino said as he introduced the two to each other. The duo dapped fists and proceeded on with B.I.

Freedom pulled the tightly wrapped package out, handed it over to Stretch, received the ten thousand, five hundred dollars and said in a sarcastic tone, "This shit better not be counterfeit."

The trio laughed and Stretch gave Freedom and Nino a handshake and a hug. Then he bounced. Freedom stared at Nino, counted out five hundred dollars, handed it to him, and asked, "You good?"

"I'm good. That should be every three days, four at the latest," Nino assured Freedom that Stretch would be back to buy more.

"Yo, I got something to take care of. I'll get at you later. Do you want to hang out?" Freedom asked, as he walked outside and gave Nino a pound with his fist. Before Nino could answer, Free continued, "Maybe we'll got to Club Speed or something."

"That's cool. Get at me later," Nino stated. He walked back through the apartment doors.

Freedom hoped back inside of his sports car and proceeded uptown. He went to pick up the watch he had on layaway. He adjusted the volume on his radio from the steering wheel, then he called Havoc.

Ring! Ring!

"What's up?" Havoc answered.

"Yo, what's hood, kid? I got that seventy-five thou for you. I'm going to the club tonight though, but when are you trying to get up?" Freedom asked as he searched for a parking spot on Broadway.

"Yo, meet me at the 40/40 around 9:30. Bring it there and I'll tell you about our next job," Havoc said, then hung up.

Freedom parked, exited the car and walked up Broadway. He entered the crowded jewelry store on 143rd Street and looked at all the store clerks hoping to see the Dominican lady who helped him days before. She was nowhere in sight so he purchased the Frank Mueller watch from another clerk and headed back to his apartment on Malcolm X Boulevard.

Meanwhile...

Out in Brooklyn, Havoc was holding a meeting with a bunch of bank investors. After the meeting, they all left the small office of the construction building in which he worked. One of the investors remained behind.

"So, out in Alpine, New Jersey, you say there's a house with five million dollars worth of diamonds in it?" Havoc asked, as he lit the investor's cigar for him.

"Yeah, but he has people looking after the house for him." The bank investor wanted Freedom to be careful because if something went wrong, shit just might come back on him.

"So he has the jewels in his daughter's bedroom in a stash spot underneath the hardwood floor?" Havoc asked as he looked over the map of the mansion. His question was more like a statement of which he needed a little clarification.

"Yeah, right there," the bank investor pointed to a location on the map, then added, "Yo, don't fuck this up, Havoc. This could be two-and-a-half million dollars a piece for us."

"Don't worry," Havoc stated. He exited the office and thought to himself, *How can I get rid of this dude? I need the whole five million.*

Havoc was startled when the investor yelled, "Havoc, you forgot the map." He handed the map to Havoc which was inside a briefcase.

"Damn, I'm buggin," Havoc stated. He grabbed the brief-case, placed it inside the trunk of his car, got in the driver's side and drove off.

Chapter 13

reedom and Nino arrived at the 40/40 Club around 9:15. Freedom scanned the area, but there was no sign of Havoc.

"Damn, kid, look at that ass," Nino spoke loudly over the music. He pointed to a chick that was leaning inside the window of a money green S500 Mercedes with 22 inch chrome rims.

"Now that's a hustler's dream," Freedom admired the big body Benz, then he said, "Damn, that's my shortie Pam." At first he didn't recognize her, but a second look at that wide ass suddenly reminded him of the time they spent together.

"Word? She got a nice body. You need to slide me that number," Nino suggested playfully.

"Yo, come here, Ms. Ross," Freedom shouted out of his car window. He flicked his headlights on and off to get Pam's attention.

"Wait a minute," Pam screamed and proceeded to walk toward Freedom.

"What's good. I see I haven't received a phone call from you in a minute," Freedom stated. He placed both of his hands on the steering wheel.

"I know you wasn't waiting around for *my* call, either,"

Pam said with her hand on her hip and a wiggle of her neck.

"I heard Jigga Man was going to be having some kind of party tonight," Nino added.

Freedom looked at Pam and added, "I see you made a pretty big catch."

"Oh, that's some dude from Brooklyn. I know *you're* not tripping over that," Pam responded. She backed away from the car and raised her eyebrows, then added, "I'll see you inside."

Pam paced back over to the money green Benz and said, "I'm sorry. That's this dude I know named Freedom." She leaned back inside of the window.

"Damn, that's the dude I'm waiting on," Havoc yelled, then flicked his headlight on and off.

"Damn, what's that bird doing?" Nino stated as he noticed the headlights.

"I don't know, but I'm going to see what's popping," Freedom said as he got out of the B.M.W. He walked in the direction of Pam.

The duo walked toward the big luxury sedan. As they got closer, Freedom noticed it was Havoc. Havoc exited the car and gave Freedom their customary handshake.

"Damn, Kikko, you riding real big in Manhattan tonight," Freedom laughed. He smirked and shook his head.

"I told you I had something crazy wild." Havoc assured Freedom that his Benz was *all that*.

"I see you met Ms. Ross," Freedom remarked.

"Yeah, I'm taking her home tonight," Havoc said and winked his eye at Pam.

They all proceeded inside the sports bar. Nino tapped Freedom and said, "I'm next."

They all admired Pam's butt then the trio was escorted to

the VIP area where they drank bottles of champagne, discussed the heist in New Jersey *and* future plans. It was midnight when Nino said "Damn, it's about time to see what *Speed* has for us."

"Yeah, you're right. Let's get up out of here," Freedom said. He got up and told Havoc to come with him with a wave of his hand.

"What's good?" Havoc asked with his hands in the air.

"We abouts to blow this joint. You coming?" Freedom asked.

Havoc pointed in Pam's direction and said, "I'm going to blow shortie's back out. So I guess I'll get up with you tomorrow, ah-ight?" He shook Nino's hand, then gave Freedom a hug, and said, "Let's go out and get that paper that you have for me."

Freedom and Havoc separated themselves from Pam and Nino. They went to Freedom's car. Freedom opened the trunk, pulled out a shopping bag and handed Havoc the bag with the seventy-five thousand dollars in it.

The duo dapped each other. "Yo, peace, kid," Havoc said then proceeded to his car where Pam waited for him.

Freedom and Nino resumed their night at Club Speed. When they arrived, all the ladies watched them as they strutted around the club with champagne bottles. They stood in front of the bathroom and rolled up a couple of blunts.

"Yo, ain't that Mercedes?" Nino asked. He lit the cigar and took long, slow pulls.

"Damn, it's her *and* Bish," Freedom stated. He pointed Bish out to Nino.

Bish and Mercedes were walking on the opposite side of the club.

"Look, bitch, there goes Free," Mercedes informed Bish

that she couldn't flirt around. They locked eyes with one another.

"Look who this ma fucka got with him," Bish said with a disgusted look on her face. Then said, "Nino." Bish had not seen Nino since he was locked up for attempted murder on her ex-boyfriend six years ago.

"I didn't even know he was gon' be here tonight," Mercedes enunciated. She pulled Bish's arm and pranced over to where Nino and Freedom stood.

"Don't look now, but they're coming over here," Freedom said. He grabbed the blunt from Nino and took a quick drag. When the ladies were close enough, he blew smoke out and asked, "How are you ladies doing?" He kissed them both on their cheeks.

"What's up, Mercedes?" Nino asked. He shook her hand.

"How you doing, Nino?" Bish asked. She waved a fake wave and continued. "I haven't seen you in a while. You been good?" She crossed her arms and rolled her eyes.

"I've been around, trying to stay low," Nino responded. He took a hit of the weed then blew smoke in Bish's face. He added, "I've been cooling since I got out." He smiled at her.

"Let's go in V.I.P. and have some drinks," Freedom suggested. He wanted to ease the tension before it got crazy.

"We'll be up in a sec. We have to go powder our noses," Mercedes stated, then walked inside the unisex bathroom.

Freedom and Nino sat in V.I.P. and admired all the pretty girls before Mercedes and Bish came up to join them.

"Yo, kid, I'd love to share something with you," Freedom said, then he looked at his cousin and continued. "I smashed Bish off." His hand was covering his mouth as he spoke so the ladies couldn't hear him. They had just returned from the bathroom.

Nino leaned his head back and said, "You smashed Bish off? Are you crazy?" he yelled in a whisper.

"Yo, Bee, one thing led to another," Freedom tried to explain. He poured champagne into both of their glasses.

"What are you going to do now?" Nino asked as he sipped on the crystal.

"I'm not fucking her anymore. I can't do that to Mercedes. She's my little trooper," Freedom said. He noticed that the ladies were trying to peep their conversation. He added, "Yo, don't say nothing." He gave his cousin a look like "Promise me you'll be quiet."

They sat, drank, smoked and enjoyed themselves for a couple of hours. The D-J played the last song of the night and stated "This is the last song. You got fifteen minutes to get with that special person. And last call for drinks."

When Mercedes found a moment, she said, "Are you coming over my crib?" She was talking to Freedom. She grabbed his arm and placed her head on his shoulder.

"Yeah, I'm coming over," Freedom looked at Bish and Nino, then added, "I have to take Nino home first."

"I'm going to go find Tiff," Bish stated. She turned up her nose, walked away and looked for a ride home.

When the night ended, the trio climbed into the car and drove home. When they got in front of Nino's building, Freedom asked, "Are you good, kid?" He looked over at his cousin.

Nino nodded and said, "I'm good. I'll get at you later, and y'all be safe." They gave one another dap. He walked through the apartment doors, then Freedom and Mercedes headed for her apartment. Mercedes played with Freedoms ear the entire ride. Freedom thought to himself, *Damn, I hope Bish didn't say anything. I can't believe I did that.*

Mercedes and Freedom entered Mercedes' apartment, took off all their clothes, and got into her bed. Freedom adjusted his pillow and fell asleep.

"Wake up. Wake up," Mercedes tugged and slapped Freedom's body. When he wouldn't budge, she gave up and went to sleep right next to him.

Chapter 14

Freedom was awakened by the morning light that crept through Mercedes' mini blinds. He looked at his cell phone and noticed he had several voice messages. He pressed the code into his Nextel phone and listened. The first message was from Havoc.

"Yo, that bitch had the biggest ass and she sucked my dick like, *How many licks does it take?*" Havoc sang happily on the voice mail.

The second message was from Bish. Freedom walked into the bathroom and closed the door so Mercedes couldn't hear it.

"Yo, nigga, you ain't shit. You think you can play me like that, go home with Mercedes and you knew I wanted to go home with your ass. Matter of fact, you do you, but I can tell you one thing, you won't be getting no more paper on Lenox Avenue. I'm going to call the police, *you little dick nigga.*" Bish banged the phone down because Freedom heard it crash against the floor when it must've fallen from wherever it sat. He knew she was mad. He heard it in the tone of her voice, but if she *was* serious, then some major shit was about to jump off.

Freedom thought to himself, *This bitch is nuts. She gots to be bullshitting. I hope she was high when she left this message. Damn, I gots to call this bitch.* Freedom dialed Bish's number and waited for an answer.

Ring. Ring. Ring.

"Hello," answered Bish, as she yawned.

"What's really good?" Freedom asked. Before Bish could answer, he said, "I hope you was bugging when you left that message." Freedom flushed the toilet. He secured the phone between his head and shoulder while he washed his hands.

"Yo, Freedom, you can go ahead and deal with Mercedes, and also count me out on your money plans," yelled Bish.

"All of this because we fucked and I didn't take you home last night?" Freedom asked, then looked into the mirror. He had a look on his face like, *This bitch is bugging.*

"All I have to say to you is, if you got any drugs over there, you better hurry up and move them, because the police will be going over there," Bish said, then hung up the call.

Freedom exited the bathroom, put on his clothes, and started to leave. Mercedes got up and asked, "What's wrong? Why are you leaving?" She rubbed her eyes to help her focus.

"Yo, your homegirl's bugging out. She wants me to fuck her, and if I don't, she's going to call the police, and let them know about B.G.'s crib." Freedom convinced Mercedes that Bish was devious.

But since Mercedes saw how her girl and her man always looked at each other, she figured Freedom might be the one trying to hit, not Bish. So she said, "I'm going to call this bitch and see what's going on?" Mercedes wiggled her neck, climbed from underneath the covers and asked heatedly, "Where's my phone?" She fumbled through her Prada pocketbook until she found her phone.

"You know she's going to lie," Freedom tried to forewarn

Mercedes, but she was already on the phone.

Mercedes ended the call and burst into tears. She threw her cell phone at Freedom and screamed, "I hate you. I hate you."

Freedom tried to comfort her, but she continued. "Get the fuck away from me, you animal, and get out, and don't ever call me again." Mercedes dropped her head into her hands and wailed until she knew Freedom was long gone.

Freedom exited the apartment and headed for B.G.'s crib. Meanwhile...

Bish called the F.B.I. office in New York City.

Ring. Ring.

"Hello, Agent Thompson, how may I help you?" answered the federal agent.

"Hi, my name is Shabisha Ellis and I have information on a drug spot," Bish said.

"Where is the location and who is supposed to be running this so-called organization?" Agent Thompson asked, preparing to jot notes inside of his pad.

"Well, his street name is Freedom. The location is on 142nd Street and Lenox Avenue," Bish sounded like she regretted doing it.

"Well, do you know how much drugs are in there?" Agent Thompson asked. He tried to keep Bish on the phone so that he could trace her call.

"Maybe two to three kilos. I'm not sure, but he drives a blue B.M.W.," Bish stated. Then hung up the call so her number couldn't be traced.

The agent sat in silence. He went over all the information and put a team of agents on the street to see if Bish's story had any credibility.

Freedom raced uptown until he made it to his crack spot.

He exited the car and ran up to the apartment. He banged on the door and yelled, "B.G., B.G."

"What's going on, kid," B.G. asked, as he opened the door. At the same time, he handed Freedom some money.

"Yo, one of those bitches is trying to set me up. Do you have any work left?" Freedom asked. He grabbed the money and proceeded to count it.

"Yeah, we got like seven ounces left," B.G. stated, then showed Freedom the remaining work.

"We gots to close down shop for a few days to see what pops off," Freedom suggested, then looked out the window.

"Do you think she was serious?" B.G. asked. He glanced at Freedom to hear his response.

"*Do I think she's serious?*" Freedom transformed his response to the form of a question. Then he added, "This bitch is crazy wild. I gave her some good dick and now she don't now how to act," Freedom stood confused.

"We gots to get the yeyo out of here," B.G. stated. He wiped down the counters in the tiny studio apartment.

"Yo, do you know someone that'll keep it in a safe place?" Freedom asked. He looked out the window to see if he noticed anything strange.

"Damn, kid, you fucked up a million dollar block," B.G. murmured as he paced back and forth. Then he continued, "My uncle got this spot on 126th Street behind the state building".

Freedom agreed to stash the rest of the drugs at B.G.'s uncle's apartment. The duo then raced off to 126th Street. Once they arrived, Freedom let B.G. out of the car and continued to search for a parking space. He parked, got out and met B.G. at the front door of B.G.'s uncle's pad. B.G. knocked on the door with the palm of his hand. After a couple of knocks, the door went flying open. B.G.'s uncle stood 6' tall, 225 pounds. He waved the duo through the door with his hands then stated, "Youngster, close my door behind you."

They continued on to the living room of the apartment. Then B.G.'s uncle continued, "What brings you by, nephew?" He had a bewildered expression on his face because B.G. didn't visit him often, and when he did, it was always because of an emergency.

"I need a favor," B.G. stated. He sat down on the soft sofa that was covered by plastic.

"What kind of favor?" B.G.'s uncle asked. Then he spat a wad of tobacco out of his mouth into a soda bottle.

"Well, I need to stash some work over your crib for a few. I should be back tomorrow," B.G. explained. He looked at Freedom signifying to his uncle that Freedom was the *head nigga in charge*.

"As long as you pay me, because nothing comes free," B.G.'s uncle replied in a raspy voice. He stared at the both of them.

Freedom looked at B.G., then dug into his pockets and asked, "How much?" He decided not to reveal his knot until *Mr. Uncle* set a price.

"How much do you want to stash?" B.G.'s uncle asked.

"Well, seven ounces. I can hit you off with five hundred a night," Freedom suggested. He handed B.G.'s uncle five hundred dollars.

"Ahight, ahight, but don't get me into your bullshit. I ain't taking the weight for nobody," B.G.'s uncle assured.

Freedom's cell phone began to ring. Freedom answered. "What's good?" then he walked back toward the entrance.

"What's popping?" Havoc asked.

Freedom got right to it. "I got some problems. I blazed one of my girl's friends and she caught feelings, now the bitch went to the cops," Freedom explained. He covered his mouth so B.G.'s uncle couldn't hear him.

"You what!" shouted Havoc. "If it's not one thing, then it's another."

"I know, kid. This is it for me though," Freedom informed.

"So where's the bitch at? Let's merk her ass." Havoc suggested. He felt the easiest way to deal with a problem was to deal with the person causing it.

"No, are you kidding?" Freedom asked.

B.G. walked into the room where Freedom stood. He watched Freedom with a curious look. He quickly thought back to Trey's death. *I hope this nigga didn't kill Trey.*

Freedom continued. "Yo, Havoc, I'm going to get at you later, ah-ight?" He then hung up the phone.

"I hope you didn't kill Trey?" B.G. asked, as the two men exited the apartment. They walked to where Freedom's car was parked and B.G. kept his eyes on Freedom the entire time.

"What made you ask me that?" Freedom asked. He hit the automatic start and unlocked the doors to his B.M.

"Shit, I was ear hustling and I heard you speaking about killing some bitch," B.G. added. He got into the passenger side and kept talking. "Shit, I know you had to think about merking Trey before he got you if you're so quick to merk a broad."

"Yo, this is different. This bitch is trying to fuck my hustle up and get a nigga a life sentence. I refuse to sit back and let her trap me off like that," Freedom explained. He placed the big sports car in drive, crept out of the cramped parking spot, and headed for Lenox Avenue.

Little did he know that the feds had put a team of agents out on the job. They staked out the crack spot on 142nd Street and Lenox Avenue. Detective Long and his partner, Detective Smith, waited in an alley a few buildings away from B.G.'s apartment. They watched through binoculars and monitored the people that came in and out of the building. Detective Long and Detective Smith were locals from the neighborhood precinct, but when cases involving drugs were concerned, primarily crack cocaine, they would join in and assist the big boys.

Chapter 15

"What's good, kid?" Freedom was speaking to one of his customers. He hit the automatic lock and locked his car doors.

"Yo, do you have four-and-a-half for me?" the customer asked. He gave Freedom a pound with his fist.

"Yo, son, give me like an hour and I'll have that for you," Freedom assured his little man that he would be in position. He and B.G. entered the building then walked up the stairs to their crack spot.

"That must be the perps right there," Detective Smith stated as he watched the duo from his high tech binoculars.

"If it's not him, then we done came up on something else," Detective Long said while he sipped on a mug of coffee. He jotted notes down in his pad.

Inside the apartment, B.G. and Freedom paced back and forth. B.G. grabbed his glass dick and took a hit of the residue and asked, "So what are you going to do?" He blew the smoke out slow and relaxed, then added, "We gots to make another trip across town."

"Yeah, you're right," Freedom replied. He rolled a blunt full of purple haze weed, then said, "This is to relax my fucking nerves."

The duo exited the apartment, jumped inside of the large sports car and peeled off.

"Smith, there they are. Get on their trail," Detective Long stated as he pointed to show his partner the car so they could follow.

"Damn, that's a nice looking vehicle," Detective Smith complimented as he drove two car lengths behind.

"We could never afford anything like that," Detective Long said. He jotted the license plate number down and said, "He's at least eighteen years old." It was an assumption, but with so many years on the force, his assumptions almost always turned out to be correct.

Freedom and B.G. had no clue they were being trailed.

"It'll be alright. We just got to do the *via cell thing*," Freedom said. He reached for the car's lighter and lit his blunt. He blew the smoke through his nose then continued, "You heard?"

"Yeah, I feel you, kid. We gots to find another stash spot because we might look too obvious coming and going," B.G. added. He then snuggled himself into the comfortable leather seat.

"Yo, I'm going to park while *you* go and get the work, ah-ight?" Freedom said. He double parked and turned on his flashers. B.G. exited the car and ran inside of his uncle's apartment.

While the two detectives waited for what was next, they called their supervisors on the cell.

Ring. Ring.

"Hello," Chief Thompson answered.

"We think we have the drug dealers from 142nd Street and Lenox Avenue," Detective Long explained. He lit up a cigarette and threw the match outside the window, then added, "We're following them now. They're up to something."

"Stay on them," Chief Thompson said, then ended the call.

B.G. got back inside the car. The two detectives took pictures of the hand pouch B.G. carried out of the apartment with him.

"Yo, we have them now," Detective Smith said as he placed his digital camera back inside of the glove compartment. He threw the big Buick in drive and continued to follow the duo back to their crack spot.

"When we get back, park in a different location," Detective Long suggested.

Once they got back on 142nd Street and Lenox Avenue, B.G. and Freedom parked and both men exited the vehicle. They ran up to the building. B.G. went inside the building and served the customer the four-and-a-half ounces. The detectives took more pictures of the transaction and drove away. They had enough evidence to gather up a search warrant for both addresses.

Freedom walked into the crack spot along with B.G. B.G. placed a tiny piece of crack back in his glass pipe and with his free hand, he flicked a *Bic* lighter. He burned the small piece of cocaine and beamed up to Scottie. When he returned from Mars, he stated in a calm manner, "Damn, kid, this is some good shit." He took another trip to Mars and when he came back, he added, "I didn't see any police all day."

"Yeah, you're right. Maybe she was pulling my leg," Freedom assumed. He strolled to the window and peeked from the dusty mini blinds, checking to see if he noticed any unmarked squad cars. He continued, "I gots to re up." He then picked up his cell phone and called Memo. Before the phone could ring, B.G. grabbed the phone, hung it up and said, "You still got that phone? That shit is probably tapped."

"Yeah, you're right," Freedom agreed. He fumbled through

the crack of the sofas to find his *burn out* prepaid phone. He found it in the love seat. Freedom proceeded to call Memo.

Ring. Ring.

"De me," Memo answered.

"Yo, Memo, what's good. I need the same thing in the morning, around 10," Freedom suggested. He turned the brand new 25 inch television on with the remote and kicked his feet up on the table.

"I got you, young Free. Don't stand me up," Memo said in his heavy Spanish dialect.

"One," Freedom said, then hung up the call.

Freedom fell asleep and held on tight to his pockets. He knew with B.G. around, nothing was safe. Before Freedom had awakened, the detectives were back on the scene waiting to get surveillance on with their digital camcorder.

"If you park in this position, we can get them when they come out of the house," Detective Long stated, as he showed Detective Smith the location by pointing.

The detectives parked and positioned themselves in a good spot from which they could see Freedom leaving and going into the building. The officers drank coffee and ate donuts as usual until they saw Freedom exit the apartment building and flag down a cab. When Freedom entered the taxi, the cops followed close behind him.

"That's our man. I wonder what he's up to," Detective Long stated with a smirk on his face. He could already see the raise he would get. He would finally be able to afford that house on the lake.

"Yeah, that's him," Smith said. He held on tight to the steering wheel. He just liked the fact that another black teenager was about to get locked up for drugs.

"They're coming to a stop. Pull over here," Long directed.

He sipped on his hot coffee and placed the Panasonic video camera in position.

Freedom exited the cab on 140th Street and Broadway, walked up to Memo and gave him a handshake that ended with a hug. Freedom and Memo walked inside of a Spanish restaurant. Inside, they exchanged merchandise. While Freedom was exiting, he turned and said, "Yo, I'm going to relax for a minute. I think shit is hot."

"Hot! What do you mean hot?" Memo asked. He peeked out of the window to see if he saw any police.

"Fish grease hot, you feel me?" Freedom said. He grabbed a shopping bag and placed the pouch inside of it.

"Yo, I'm going on a vacation," Memo responded. He slapped Freedom on the back and added, "I suggest you do the same as well, Kikko."

Freedom jumped inside of a black Lincoln that was waiting for him to take him back to the avenue.

The detectives continued to follow a couple of car lengths behind. One of the detective's phone rang.

Ring. Ring.

"What's up?" Detective Long answered. He pressed play on the Camcorder to review the prerecorded videotape of Freedom and Memo's meeting.

"Yo, what's up Big L. I have a situation. I may need your help," the voice on the other end stated.

"Okay, speak to me, Mr. H.," Long agreed. He glanced at his partner to see if he could hear him.

"You know I don't do the phone thing, so meet me at the pier, after dark," the voice said, then hung up.

Freedom arrived on Lenox Avenue. He called B.G. from his prepaid cell phone. He told him to be ready to come out when he spotted a black Lincoln pull up. Freedom assured that it would be him. B.G. noticed the cabi from his window. He raced down the stairs and hopped in the back of the vehicle.

The duo proceeded to B.G.'s uncle's apartment to stash the brick of cocaine. Freedom felt he was being watched, so he decided that once they arrived at the stash house, B.G. would get back inside the Lincoln and go back to the avenue while he would go out the back door of B.G.'s uncle's house and catch another cab.

The idea worked as planned. Freedom went through the back door through the cut, and ended up on 127th Street. The detectives followed B.G. back to the crack spot. Freedom caught a taxi back to Malcolm X Boulevard. B.G. made it back to his apartment.

The D.T.s parked and waited to see if they could gather up more information.

"I guess that's it. The young fella must live on 126th Street," Long said, as he tucked away his equipment.

"Yeah, you're right." Smith pulled the old car out of the dark alley and said, "I'll drop you off." He proceeded to drive where Detective Long's car was parked.

The officers made it to where Long's black Honda Accord was. Detective Long gathered his belongings, and before he exited the car he said, "I'll be waiting for you tomorrow at the same place and time." He slammed the door shut and went on about his business.

Chapter 16

Havoc raced down the Westside Highway. He scanned through his long collection of hip hop CDs. He stopped at Biggie's *Life After Death*, turned the volume up to level 6 and continued to cruise down the highway. The sun had set and it was almost dark. He placed his parking lights on and turned into Chelsea's pier. Havoc's cell phone rang.

Ring. Ring.

"What's going on?" Havoc answered, as he turned his radio down. He pulled into a parking spot and cut off his lights.

"I'm about ten minutes away," the voice on the other end said.

"Ai-ight, Big L," Havoc assured he wasn't going anywhere. He hung up the call, reclined his seat all the way back, and turned his music back up.

A few minutes passed and Havoc was startled by a tap on his window. He raised his seat, turned down his radio and opened the passenger's side door.

"If it ain't Mr. H," Long said. He looked at Havoc and got into the compact car. "What brings this on? I haven't seen you in two months." Long looked at him.

"What can I say? I've been busy." Havoc stated, then he

offered Detective Long a cigar.

"No, I'm okay," Detective Long declined with a wave of the hand and said, "I can't wait to hear what you need *this* time." He raised his brow two quick times.

"I know you made out good especially when you got that Porsche for me," Havoc said. Before Long could answer, Havoc added, "You pocketed ten thousand dollars."

"Yeah, right, but I was in debt," Detective Long made it be known that he had no fun with the money.

"Yo, I got another issue. I'll need a car and a cover up. It might be a serious body count," Havoc said. He looked at his friend to make sure that he paid full attention.

"What do you mean, a body count?" Long asked. The two men locked eyes.

"I'm dealing with some bank investors and I think these cocksuckas got a plot on me," Havoc stated. He busted a cigar down the middle and dumped the tobacco out the window.

"So you want me to steal a car, then cover up whatever might happen?" Long asked. He pulled his notepad out and jotted the information down so he wouldn't forget it.

"Yeah, this is my final heist and I got some bad vibes about it," Havoc said. He licked the inside of the cigar and rewrapped it with marijuana inside of it.

"In three days, I should have something. And I should be able to make it look real good," Long assured. He reached for the door handle, then added, "But it'll cost you," Long added.

"It always does," Havoc yelled through the door before Long could close it. Afterwards, the two men went their separate ways.

Havoc and Detective Long met one afternoon in Harlem four years ago. Havoc was into the drug game at that time. He had just purchased a kilo of cocaine, he and a female companion. The female had a black knapsack around her shoulder. Detective Long had been watching the spot all day long and noticed when Havoc and the girl entered, neither of the two had a knapsack. But when they left, they were holding. Havoc opened the door to the rental car and said, "Put it in the back seat."

"Okay, baby," the female friend agreed.

They both got inside and proceeded to drive away.

This is my big break. I can get that promotion now, thought Detective Long. He raced in hot pursuit behind Havoc's car then Long pulled up alongside of Havoc and his friend. He ordered Havoc to pull over. He placed his badge and brandished his semi-automatic handgun up against his car window where Havoc could see it. Havoc looked on, scared. He led Detective Long on a ten-minute high-speed chase. Havoc dodged and weaved through traffic until he lost control of his vehicle and ended up crashing into a fire hydrant. Havoc reached for the knapsack and exited the car. Long continued the chase on foot. Due to Havoc's chronic weed habit, he immediately ran out of breath. Long caught up to him, tackled him to the ground, then slapped the handcuffs on his wrists. The detective rambled through the sack and discovered a large amount of cocaine.

"Who are you working for?" Detective Long asked. He picked up the bag *and* Havoc.

"No one," Havoc shouted. He looked up at the cop.

"This is your lucky day then, kid. I'm going to let you go, but you have to split the profit 50/50," Long suggested. He used his handcuff key and unlocked them from around Havoc's wrist.

"What did you say?" Havoc asked. He stood and looked at the police officer in amazement.

"Take it or leave it," Detective Long said.

Long looked around to make sure no one witnessed what went down. Havoc then gave Long a number where he could be reached.

"What about the car?" Havoc stuttered. Before he could say anything else, Detective Long assured him that he would take care of it. "Run along. I'll clean it up."

Detective Long cleaned up the scene of the crime like he had promised. He filled out a report that stated something about a stolen car and that the driver had gotten away on foot.

Four years later, Detective Long and Havoc still stayed in contact. Their drug business had gotten too risky so they changed their hustle to heisting. Long agreed that he would help Havoc gather information on locations, plus provide him with any tools he would need to make the jobs successful. He also suggested that Havoc find a partner to assist him, and that his partner must know nothing about their relationship.

Chapter 17

Freedom arrived back at his apartment and realized that his mom was home. He raced up the stairs to his bedroom and plotted on his next move about how he could still get money from the drug game. Freedom lay back on his bed and adjusted his pillow. He fell asleep. A few hours later, he was awakened by the beep from his new Frank Mueller watch. He checked the time, then fumbled through the sheets in search of his cell phone. He noticed he had one voice message. He gently tapped his code into his cell and waited to hear the voice of the messenger. It was from his number one runner, B.G.

"Yo, kid, 9 o'clock in the morning. I got this dude; he wants nine of them things. He don't know the prices, so you make up your own prices. Holla back." B.G. let his boss know that it would be on and cracking, and for him to be ready.

Freedom cleared the message. He stared into space and thought to himself, *Damn, that's it. I'll get another prepaid phone and hustle via cell. Fuck that block shit. I'll whip up over B.G.'s uncle's crib and it's a go.* He was startled from the vibration of his cell. It was another call. He answered, "Yo, what's hood?"

"Yo, kid, where you at? The kid will be coming through in a minute," B.G. announced.

"Yo, meet me over your uncle's in like a half," Freedom stated. He was on his way to brush his teeth.

"Don't have me waiting over there forever," B.G. added, then hung up.

Meanwhile, Detective Long and Detective Smith were in position at 126th Street. Long pulled out all of his toys—his pencil, his notepad, his video camera, and his coffee. Smith waited patiently behind the steering wheel. With both of his hands, he gripped the wheel tightly, pulled himself up close, watched the scene through the steering wheel, and stated, "We should call the boss." He glanced at his partner then added, "To see if that search warrant came back from Washington, D.C."

"We should give it some time, because when we get one more transaction, it'll stick," Long suggested as he prepared the videotape.

"Look, look, there goes the old man coming up the street," Detective Smith pointed and motioned with his coffee mug.

Long placed the camcorder barely over the dashboard and zoomed in on B.G. then stated, "He's at the door."

"Yo, we should really call the boss now so we can make the bust," Detective Smith suggested.

He picked up his cell phone, but before he could place the call, Long grabbed the phone and said, "Wait a minute, there goes the blue B.M."

"Maybe you're right," Smith agreed. He placed the phone back at the center console and kept his eyes glued to B.G.

"I know I'm right," Long added. He kept his hand steady and sipped on his hot coffee. "They're not onto us. They think this is a safe spot," Long offered his opinion.

Freedom entered the apartment, shook B.G.'s uncle's hand and said, "I'll have the five hundred dollars for you when we finish and come back." He nodded to emphasize his statement.

"Don't worry. Take your time," B.G.'s uncle stated and showed B.G. where he had some baking soda.

"Yo, the kid wants nine, so we'll whip up two hundred grams then stretch it to two-fifty," B.G. suggested. He looked at Freedom and said, "I gots to get my cut," he said rubbing his hands together as if they were cold. He even emphasized his enthusiasm by blowing on his hands while he rubbed them together.

"Do you, kid," Freedom responded. He walked over to the window and stared out to see if he saw any five-O.

"Free, Free, come here," B.G. yelled. He wanted Freedom to help him bag up the work in zip lock bags.

"Who's this kid anyways?" Freedom asked, as he weighed and dumped each ounce into individual plastic bags.

"Some kid from the Bronx," B.G. answered. He continued to stir the baking soda into the cocaine until it got harder and larger. Then he added, "Yo, this shit should bring him back."

The duo finished their chefing skills and proceeded to meet the kid that wanted the work. They got into the car and peeled off. Close behind, the two detectives followed.

"Yo, watch out for the pot holes," Detective Long said. He tried to keep a steady hand on the video camera.

"Don't worry about me," Smith stated. He looked at his partner to make sure he kept a steady hand, then added, "Just keep focused."

"149th Street and Broadway. Turn down 149th and look for a red LS430," B.G. assured Freedom that the car should be in place.

"Is this dude driving a red car?" Freedom asked. He looked over at B.G. who sat snuggled on the passenger's side. "It's crazy hot. I'll let you out and you give it to him and tell him to give me sixty-five hundred, ah-ight?"

Just as planned, the Lexus sat parked on 149th Street between Broadway and Amsterdam Avenue. Freedom parked on the Amsterdam Avenue side.

"What do you think they're doing?" Smith asked. He parked where his partner could get a good shot of what they were up to.

"I don't know, but whatever it is, I'm ready for it," Long stated as he chewed on a ham sandwich.

"Didn't your mama teach you not to talk with your mouth full?" Smith asked in a sarcastic tone of voice.

"Oh, I'm sorry," Long apologized. He continued to talk with his mouth full. He placed the camera in position, then zoomed in on the back window of Freedom's car. The two detectives waited.

B.G. exited the car and proceeded to walk down the block. He held on tight to a purple *Crown Royal* bag that contained the nine ounces of crack. He stopped at the red car, tapped on the glass and got into the passenger's side seat. The man gave B.G. a brown paper bag that contained sixty-five hundred dollars.

"Is it all there?" the kid asked. He looked at B.G. and pointed to the Crown Royal bag.

"I should be asking you the same thing," B.G. smiled and exited the car. He leaned into the window and stated, "When you finish, holla back."

"Take down the number to those plates," stated Smith, then pointed to the red Lexus.

"Yeah, we can get a two for one," Long suggested. He jotted the numbers down, then closed his video camera and told his partner, "They're leaving. Catch up."

The detectives followed behind Freedom and B.G. They continued until they got to 142nd Street and Lenox Avenue. They parked and walked inside B.G.'s crack spot.

"I don't know what these guys are up to, but they're definitely drug dealers," Long stated. He jotted a couple of notes down then propped his feet up on the dashboard.

"I'm going to call the boss and see what's up with that warrant," Smith said. He picked up his cell phone and called the station.

Ring. Ring.

"Hello," Chief Thompson answered. He swung his office chair around and grabbed the search warrant for the 126th Street apartment complex off of his desk. He said, "Smith, I thought you guys would've been calling."

"How did you know it was me?" Smith asked.

"That's what we have caller I.D. for." Thompson assured him if it wasn't for the caller I.D., he wouldn't have known.

"So do you have the search warrant?" Smith asked. He looked at Long, shook his head up and down and smiled, then continued. "For 126th Street, correct?"

"Yeah, we got it. So in the morning, go pay them fucking dealers a little visit," Thompson said then hung up the cell.

"In the morning we have to gear up and raid the spot," Detective Smith gave Long the good news.

"That's good. So it's a wrap for today. Take me to my car," Long said, then thought, *Damn, where can I come up with a car in that neighborhood? Alpine, New Jersey.*

The two men raced down the Westside Highway to where Long's car was. Once they arrived, Long exited the car with all of his gadgets and told his partner, "I'll see you tomorrow," before he closed the car door. He added, "We have a big day ahead of us." He closed the door and proceeded to his car.

Chapter 18

R ing. Ring. Ring.

"What's popping?" Freedom asked as he answered his phone.

"How are you doing?" Mercedes asked, then said, "I spoke with Bish and she told me everything."

"Everything like what?" Freedom took a long pull on a cigar that he rolled earlier.

"She told me she called the feds. She gave them your address to your block, plus she said that they told her they would be on top of it," Mercedes explained.

"She is crazy as hell. She fucked up my whole issue," Freedom said as he continued to suck the smoke in from the weed blunt. He blew it out slowly.

"I know, but you should've thought about that before you stuck your dick in her," Mercedes barked. She wiggled her neck and raised her eyebrows.

"Yo, Mercedes, I told you I was sorry for what I did. I mean, it's her fault as well as mine," Freedom apologized. He got up from the couch and proceeded to look out the window. He continued, "Yo, baby, I'll call you later to give you some info in case I get knocked."

"I didn't say I was going to stand by your side in this," Mercedes reminded Freedom that she was still upset, then she added, "I'll be waiting on your call."

"Ah-ight, baby," Freedom said. He dumped the ashes to the blunt and took another pull. As he blew the smoke out, he asked her, "Do you still love me?"

"*Do I still love you?*" Mercedes turned her answer to the form of a question.

"Yo, I'm going to come over your crib later about ten o'clock, ah-ight? Then you can tell me," Freedom stated. He flopped down in the comfortable couch.

"Ah-ight, but just to talk." Mercedes assured him that it wouldn't be any monkey business, then hung up the call.

"Yo, B.G.," Freedom yelled through the tiny apartment. He sat on the couch dazed from the purple haze blunt.

"What's up, kid?" B.G. asked. He proceeded to walk into the living room where Freedom sat.

"Yo, that bitch really did tell them crackers where we hustle at," Freedom said. He locked eyes with B.G.

"Damn, kid," B.G. shook his head from side to side. He then reached for the roach of the cigar with his thumb and index finger. He added, "So what are we going to do?"

"I'm thinking about buying another phone then we just hustle off of them shits," Freedom summed up.

"So what do we do in the meantime?" B.G. asked. He took four quick hits off the roach and dropped it into the ashtray.

"We fall back and see what happens," Freedom said. He then grabbed his cell and keys and proceeded to walk out the door.

"Where are you going?" B.G. asked. He stood in the middle of the living room with his arms opened.

"I'm going to this chick's crib and in the morning, we'll go and cook up the rest of that shit," Freedom answered, then gave B.G. the peace sign with his middle and index fingers.

Freedom jumped inside of his car and proceeded to go to Mercedes' apartment. He dodged and weaved through traffic until he arrived in front of her building. Freedom searched for a place to park. He found a parking spot two buildings up the block. He parked, got out and waited for someone to leave out of the security doors where an old man and lady held the doors open until he grabbed it. He raced up the stairs to Mercedes' floor, stood in front of her door, placed his hand over the peep-hole and knocked.

"Who is it?" Mercedes asked. She looked through the peep-hole but couldn't see anything. Then she yelled, "Who the fuck is it covering up my peephole?"

"Open the door," Freedom bellowed. He covered his mouth with his other hand so she couldn't hear his laughter.

"Why you playing for?" Mercedes yanked the door open and placed her hand on her waist and hip, then added, "I knew it was your ass anyway," she smiled.

Freedom walked through the doorway and closed the door behind him. He grabbed Mercedes from the back of her head and pulled her close then stuck his tongue inside of her mouth and gave her a French kiss. He asked, "Do you love me?"

"Yes, baby," Mercedes said and smiled from ear to ear.

"I told you I was coming." He sat down on Mercedes' sofa.

"I knew you were," Mercedes said as she curled up beside him and placed her head in between Freedom's arm and chest. "Just don't leave me any more."

Freedom kissed Mercedes on her neck. He smelled her scent as he trimmed her upper body with his nose. Then Mercedes placed her hand around his neck and licked Freedom's neck and ears with her tongue. The young couple took each other's clothes off. Excited and short of breath, Freedom said, "Baby, I won't ever fuck this up again."

He placed himself in between Mercedes' legs and spread them as wide as he could. He fumbled around her private area until he found the soft juicy entrance to her body then placed his brick hard dick inside of her. He pumped slowly, out and in, and made circular motions with his butt and hips.

"Baby, I missed you," Mercedes sighed then pumped back and grabbed Freedom's butt. She continued. "Fuck me, harder, harder."

"Like that, Boo?" Freedom asked. He tried to keep up to Mercedes' rhythm.

Mercedes squirmed and scratched Freedom's back with her nails, then gently nibbled on his neck. She whispered inside of his ear, "I'm cumming, baby. Please don't stop."

"Cum for Daddy," Freedom sounded confident, as he looked down into Mercedes' brown eyes. With her legs up in the air above her head, she squinted her eyes as her leg shook. She screamed and moaned, "I'm cumming. I'm cumming."

Freedom pumped faster and harder until he came. He flopped down on her and uttered, "Damn, I missed that."

They locked eyes then Freedom said, "You know, what your friend did could cost me to go to prison for a long time."

"Yeah, I know, baby, I'm sorry," Mercedes replied. She grabbed Freedom so he couldn't get up.

"I want you to promise me something," Freedom said, as he stroked through her hair.

"What is it, baby?" Mercedes asked. She looked confused.

"Well, you know my moms is a good lady, and she might not handle me being in jail, so I got this safe with about two to three hundred grand in it, and a gun," Freedom explained. He finally got up from Mercedes' hold then continued. "I'm going to give you the combination to it, so give her a hundred and fifty thousand dollars and you take the rest, but you have to promise me, you won't fuck me."

"I promise," Mercedes agreed. She walked to the bathroom. She looked at Freedom to see if he was looking.

"I'm serious. I might go to prison for a while if those feds catch me out there." Freedom assured that he was in some deep shit. He looked at Mercedes' butt cheeks rock side to side with a slight case of cellulite, then added, "And you better not give my pussy to anybody."

"Don't worry about that," Mercedes said as she returned with a hot and soapy bathcloth. She then proceeded to wipe Freedom's nuts and the head of his dick off. She placed her hot mouth around his penis and proceeded to suck it. She looked into Freedom's eyes and added, "Now it's clean."

"The combination to my safe is ...,"

Freedom started to give her the number, but Mercedes interrupted. "If you don't feel you want me to have any money, then I'll give it all to your mama."

"Don't bug out. I told you what to do," Freedom assured her that that was his plan.

"So what's the combination?" Mercedes asked as she wiggled her Baby Phat panties around her hips and butt.

"It's 0-2-15," Freedom stated. Then he proceeded to put his clothes back on. "Don't go over there unless I tell you too," he added.

"Ah-ight, baby, don't worry," Mercedes assured she wouldn't go over to his crib unless he told her to.

Freedom gave her a kiss, then exited the apartment. He raced down the stairs and out of the building. He jumped inside of his car and peeled off. He arrived in front of his apartment building on Malcolm X Boulevard and called B.G., then proceeded inside.

Ring. Ring.

"Hello," B.G. answered with a crackle in his voice.

"What's hood?" Freedom asked, then lay back on his couch.

"Everything is everything," B.G. assured he was ah-ight and hadn't seen any cops. "This kid from Trey's projects wants a biggie," he remembered to inform his homie.

"Word. Well, in the morning, meet me over your uncle's, ah-ight?" Freedom said as he was startled by his mother when she entered the house.

"Well, let me go back to what I was doing," B.G. stated, then ended the call.

Freedom kissed his mother on the forehead and raced up to his bedroom to count out his money. He rewrapped the two hundred seventy thousand dollars in rubber bands and placed it back inside his safe, then went to bed.

Chapter 19

Detective Long and his partner, Detective Smith, waited inside of the precinct for the search warrant they needed for Freedom's crack spot. They needed to see who was assigned to assist them on the raid. Chief Thompson walked out of his office. Then he motioned for the detectives to come in. Thompson stared at both of his subordinates and handed Smith the warrant to the 126th Street building complex. He announced, "I have Detective Reid and Detective Jackson on the bust as well." He sat down in his office chair, placed both of his hands on his desk and pulled himself close. Then he added, "Look you two, don't screw this up." He was pointing at Long and Smith.

"Don't worry, boss. We got your best two detectives on this with us. *We can't go wrong,*" Detective Long stated in a sarcastic tone.

"I hope you don't make them look bad," Chief Thompson murmured.

The detectives exited the office and left the building. They got into separate cars. Long, Smith, Reid and Jackson drove the unmarked cars to 126th Street. They had on police jackets, and underneath were their bulletproof vests. Each of them had semi-automatic handguns. They arrived on 126th Street, parked on the side of the state building and spoke on their walkie talkies to each other.

Like any other morning, Freedom drove down the street in search of a parking spot. He found a spot and five minutes later, B.G. walked from around the corner. He entered the apartment with Freedom close behind him.

"What's good?" Freedom asked as he gave B.G.'s uncle five hundred dollars. "Here's an extra hundred. Go get me a prepaid phone from the corner store."

"And get me some cigarettes," B.G. added before his uncle could walk out the door.

"Yo, let's hook up them nine joints," Freedom said as he pulled the drugs out of the stash spot.

"I'm already on top of it," B.G. stated. He placed the pot on the stove then added, "I need a fucking eye opener anyway."

The duo did their usual technique. They stretched the cocaine into crack, and bagged the crack into one zip lock bag. They weighed all two hundred and fifty grams and placed it inside of the bag.

"Damn, that was quick." Freedom glanced at his watch.

"Yeah, twenty minutes." B.G. assured him he knew what he was doing. He placed a small piece of crack into his pipe, stared at Freedom with his eyes opened wide and took a hit.

"Yo, Smith, that old ma fucka ain't coming back no time soon." Reid assured the others that it was time for them to act on the raid.

"Yeah, you're right. Long and I will go in through the front entrance while you and Jackson handle the rear." Smith agreed.

The detectives raced across the crowded street and just like they planned it, Detectives Long and Smith burst through the front door.

"Police! Police, get down! Don't nobody move," the detectives yelled from the back entrance and the front.

Jackson and Reid searched the apartment while Smith and Long read B.G. and Freedom their rights.

B.G. and Freedom lay on the cold kitchen floor. They looked at each other and shook their heads from side to side. Freedom looked at the officers and said in a nervous tone, "Damn, that bitch got me fucked up."

"If it ain't Freedom, the Kingpin of the City," Long stated as he searched Freedom's pockets. Then he added, "Damn, that's a lot of coke. If I didn't know any better I would say this is a laboratory."

"It is," laughed the rest of the detectives. Then they picked the duo up off of the floor after handcuffing them.

"Whose house is this?" Reid asked as he continued to destroy the apartment.

"Here, take these ma fuckas and place them into the car," Long suggested.

Jackson and Smith proceeded to go outside. Once outside, they noticed a crowd of people and blue and whites with their flashers on. The patrolmen directed traffic. The detectives placed B.G. and Freedom into separate cars. The other officers continued to search the apartment and bagged and sealed the crack for evidence. Once the detectives were finished, Long and Smith took Freedom while Jackson and Reid took B.G. down to the precinct. When they arrived at the station, they placed the duo inside of a cold holding cell that contained only a cement bench and a toilet.

It was a while before they were fingerprinted. Once fingerprinted and mug shots were taken, they were placed back inside of the cell to be questioned later.

They placed B.G. inside of a room with a table, two chairs

and a long mirror on the wall, where one could see in but not out.

"So, what's going on, Mr. Ward?" Reid asked. He paced around the tight room with his fist on his chin.

"Do you want to tell me what you're doing here?" Jackson asked, as he sat in the chair right in front of B.G.

"I have no idea. I was visiting a relative and you guys showed up," B.G. explained. Then he glanced at Jackson to see if the detective believed his story.

"Wrong answer," Reid yelled as he banged on the table. He locked eyes with B.G. to show him he meant business then added, "You're in *my* ma fucking city, feeding *my* people this poison. That's why *you're* here," he yelled.

"I don't have any clue what you're talking about," B.G. said. He took a deep swallow of his spit.

"Look, Mr. Ward, we can play these little games, but a couple of weeks ago a man was kidnapped on 140th Street right down the block from your house. The guy turned up dead, so please, tell me you got answers," Jackson assured he would try his best to stick B.G. and Freedom with the murder.

"I knew him, but I have no idea what happened to him," B.G. said as he looked at Trey's picture.

"Ah-ight, play hardball, but you're looking at a lot of time," Reid stated. He then escorted B.G. back to his cell.

"Yo, kid, this shit is serious. These ma fuckas trying to pin that Trey shit on us too," B.G. explained to Freedom.

"They're what? Come on, kid, that's bullshit." Freedom jumped up and banged on the wall. "You didn't tell them anything, did you?" Freedom was shook.

"Yo, son, I don't know anything about Trey." B.G. tried to calm his boss' nerves.

Before the duo could finish their conversation, Detective

Smith and Detective Long placed Freedom in handcuffs and took him into the same interrogation room. Smith uncuffed him and stated, "Yo, kid, I don't know how much money you have or how old you are, but you're in some deep shit."

"Deep shit?" Freedom reformed his answer into a question then locked eyes with the detective and stated, "It looks like I'm in a police station to me."

"Come on, kid, cut the jokes. You're facing twenty years in prison, and my buddies are trying to say that you and your partner know something about a murder," Long stated then sipped on a cup of hot coffee. "It looks like you're headed for a life behind bars," he added.

"I want to contact my lawyer," Freedom suggested, then glanced at the two detectives.

"Do you know this guy?" Long asked. He pushed Trey's picture across the table.

"I told you I want to see my lawyer." Freedom assured he wouldn't be answering any questions without his attorney being present.

"Well, being that you want to play hardball, I'll see you when you get arraigned," Long stated. He signaled for a plain-clothes cop to take Freedom back to the holding cell. "I'll be here if you change your mind," the detective yelled down the hall.

Once Freedom was placed back inside the cold holding cell, he flopped down beside B.G. and said, "Yo, B., if you make it to the streets before me, holla at Cedes for me. Tell her I said to contact my moms."

"Don't worry, kid, I got you," B.G. tried to comfort his friend.

"Mr. Ward, get yourself together. You're about to go in front of the judge," a uniformed officer yelled. He opened the steel door and ordered for B.G. to turn around and place his hands behind his back. The officer handcuffed B.G. and proceeded to take him to the courtroom.

The judge looked B.G. up and down, read him his charges and then granted him bond. B.G. had to be released to a guardian *and* his probation officer. Then he would be placed on house arrest for the remainder of the pre-trial. The officer brought B.G. back to where Freedom waited, then ordered Freedom to turn around and placed him in a set of handcuffs. He took him to see the same judge. The judge read Freedom his charges and denied him bond. She stated that he was a flight risk. She also asked him if he wanted a court-appointed lawyer.

"Court appointed," Freedom stated. He was trembling. Freedom was marched back to the holding cell where he waited to talk to his new lawyer. He stood in front of B.G. and asked B.G., "Did she grant you a bond?"

"Yeah, but I have to call my mom. She has to come up with the probation officer in the morning to come get me," B.G. was smiling.

"Shit, these crackers didn't give me a bond. They said that I was a flight risk, then the bitch said that I was facing fifteen years to life," Freedom said. He paced around the tiny cell.

"I'll be meeting my lawyer in a minute, so I'ma tell him to holla at mom dukes," B.G. sounded excited.

"Yo, don't forget me, dog," Freedom stated and watched as B.G. was escorted to see his lawyer.

"Mr. Lewis, your lawyer is ready for you also," the uniformed officer told Freedom. He escorted him to see his court-appointed lawyer as well.

Chapter 20

"There it is," the bank investor said as he showed Havoc their next heist.

"*Damn, this dude must have some real paper,*" Havoc wondered. He looked at his buddy then adjusted his fitted cap.

The two men watched the location of their heist. They analyzed every person that went in and out of the huge mansion.

"Yo, there he is right there," the investor pointed and sunk himself low into the driver's seat so he couldn't be seen.

"This dude is driving a Mercedes Benz CLK," Havoc said, then he watched the man enter the house. Havoc looked at his partner and continued, "In two days, it's on."

"We've seen enough. Let's get out of here," the investor suggested. He placed the car in drive and drove away slowly.

"Yeah, I gots to get back to Brooklyn," Havoc stated. Then he looked out the back window and made sure no one had noticed them.

The duo finally made it back to Brooklyn.

"Where do you want to go?" the investor asked. He looked at Havoc and waited for an answer.

"Take me to the construction site," Havoc suggested.

"Yo, Havoc, this is real big, so we need this to work. It's

five million dollars in it for us," the investor assured. He parked outside of the construction company.

Havoc opened the car door and got out. Before he closed the door he stated, "As long as your information is precise, we shouldn't have any problems." He then closed the door and proceeded inside the building.

Once inside, Havoc walked through the main office door, sat in the soft black leather chair, picked his cell phone up and called Detective Long.

Ring. Ring. Ring.

"Hello," Detective Long answered in a country tone of voice.

"Yo, what's up, Big L?" Havoc asked. He kicked his feet up on the desk and leaned back in the chair.

"What's going on with the situation?" Long asked, then walked down the hall of the precinct so no one could hear.

"Well, I know where the crib is, and I know all of the cars that're usually parked there," Havoc assured he was on top of things.

"Well, later on, around 8:30, I should have a vehicle for you, so contact me, ah-ight?" Long stated. He sat on the edge of the steps.

"I'll be there, the same spot as usual. Don't be late," Havoc assured he would be in position.

"*Don't be late?* I'm never late," Long answered. He noticed his partner coming from afar so he said, "I have to go. I'll be there at 8:30." He ended the call.

Havoc stared into the air and thought to himself, *I gots to come up with a plan to destroy Tommy (the bank investor).* When Havoc came back from outer space, he decided to call Freedom. He searched through his Nextel phone for Freedom's number, then he pressed the automatic dial button.

Ring. Ring. Ring. Ring. Ring.

Damn, where is this little dude? Havoc asked himself. He hung up the call. He took another trip to Mars and when he came back this time, he called Pam.

Ring. Ring.

"Hello," Pam answered. She told her friends to quiet down by putting her index finger on her sexy lips.

"What's up, baby?" Havoc asked. He walked up to the main entrance and made sure the door was locked. Then he continued, "How have you been?"

"I haven't heard from you in a while. Where have *you* been hiding?" Pam asked. She walked into her bedroom away from her friends.

"I've been around, taking care of mad business, you know," Havoc assured he was busy.

"Well, what did I do to deserve this call?" Pam asked, as she sat on the edge of her king size bed. Her insides got wet just hearing Havoc's voice.

"I wanted to know if you've heard from Freedom?" Havoc asked as he proceeded back to the comfortable office chair. Then he said, "I haven't heard from this dude all day."

"I don't talk to him like that. We just do business," Pam said.

"Let me ask you a question," Havoc grabbed a pen from the desk along with a pad, then continued, "Do you know his government name?"

"I think it's Reggie Lewis," Pam wasn't a hundred percent sure. Then she asked, "Why?"

"He called me with a situation the other day and I don't know if he's ah-ight or not," Havoc explained as he jotted Freedom's real name down.

"Well, when are we getting up again?" Pam asked. She wasn't trying to hear anything else about Freedom. Havoc had her open and she was trying to get up with him whenever she could.

"If you're available tonight, then it's a go," Havoc responded. He then put the pen and the piece of paper in his pocket.

"I'll give you a call later and let you know," Pam stated. She proceeded to go back into the room with her guests then she concluded, "Okay, baby?" and ended the call.

Havoc once again thought to himself. *I know this fool hasn't gotten himself arrested. Let me call around and check.* For hours, he called around the entire Gotham City, Federal and state, trying to see if his partner in crime was arrested. Every number he dialed, they told him nothing. Freedom's name hadn't been logged in the computer as of yet. Then Havoc stared into space and revisited Mars. He thought, *He must be on the low, or he ditched his old cell phone.* He came back to earth and decided he would prepare himself for his meeting with Mr. Long.

Chapter 21

"Come in, Mr. Lewis," the court-appointed attorney said. He motioned to the uniformed officer to take the handcuffs off of Freedom. Then he continued. "Have a seat, make yourself comfortable, and by the way, my name is Mike Holms." He reached out to shake Freedom's hand.

"How are you doing?" Freedom asked as he grabbed the lawyer's hand tightly. He trembled as he sat in the cold wooden chair.

"Let's see here, Mr. Lewis," Mr. Holms stated as he looked over the indictment. "It looks like you're up to your neck in this shit." He glanced at Freedom through his gold framed reading glasses.

"So what does it look like for me, Mike," Freedom asked. He locked eyes with the attorney.

"Well, it says here that you're charged with having two hundred and fifty grams of (crack) cocaine base and seven hundred and fifty grams of powder cocaine," Mr. Holms stated, as he searched through the paperwork. He then continued. "The cocaine base is what's going to kill you. You're looking at fifteen years alone with just that."

"Damn," Freedom stated as he shook his head back and forth.

"But, there is a way that you can help yourself," the lawyer assured that Freedom could help himself out. Then he explained, "There's this departure called 5K1.1" He glanced into freedom's eyes, adjusted his glasses, then continued. "You can provide substantial information to the agents and they'll help you get home quicker."

Freedom looked on. He thought to himself, *I have to get back on the streets. Damn, I can't believe this bitch got me by the balls in this situation.* He snapped out of his thought when he noticed Detectives Long and Smith standing in the doorway. Then he said, "I'm ready to tell what I know."

"Come in fellas," Mr. Holms motioned to the detectives with a wave of his hand.

"Hi, what's going on?" Detective Smith greeted the lawyer with a handshake.

"I think he's ready to speak to you guys," Mr. Holms assured.

"So we'll get the prosecutor and type up some agreements," Long stated as he proceeded to walk out of the office.

"So, if I tell you what I know, I go home, right?" Freedom sounded confused as he stared at the detectives.

"Well, nothing is promised, but if it's good, you might get a motion from the U.S. attorney's office recommending that you get a time cut," Detective Smith explained.

"Yeah," Mr. Holms agreed as he sat with his legs crossed and his hands clasped tightly together.

After fifteen minutes had passed, Detective Long along with Prosecutor Hill and Long's boss, Chief Thompson, walked through the office door and greeted each other. They all sat down and began to ask Freedom questions.

"So, my name is Chief Thompson," Thompson introduced himself to Freedom. "I hear you may have some valuable information for us."

"I don't know how much it'll help me, but I have a mother on the outside that I have to help out," Freedom explained that he was only doing it so he could continue helping out his mother with the bills.

"So what is it that you have that is so valuable?" Mr. Hill asked. He sat directly in front of Freedom.

"Wait a minute," Chief Thompson interrupted. He placed his hands on the table and said, "Who are you working for?"

"I work for myself," Freedom spoke. He took a deep swallow.

"So, do you now this man?" Detective Long showed Freedom a picture of Tremaine.

Freedom's eyes widened. He knew that if he told them what really happened to Trey that he might get off lightly, so he quickly answered, "Yes."

"Where do you know him from?" Long asked. He looked at his partners and handed Smith a pad so he could take notes.

"Wait a minute," Mr. Holms interrupted. He looked at his client and his colleagues, then added, "We have to have him sign the cooperation papers first."

"Ah-ight," Mr. Hill laughed, then showed Freedom and his attorney the papers to sign.

Freedom signed the documents without reading them over. "Now, let us know what you know about the guy in the picture," Chief Thompson said.

"Well, me and that guy Tremaine, we were in competition, and he threatened me," Freedom answered. He glanced at his audience. Then he continued. "Now this other guy I do business with agreed to kill him before Tremaine ended up killing me."

"So what happened," Long asked as he jotted down notes in his pad.

"He killed him for me. He went and shot him so we could continue doing our business," Freedom stated. He sat back and sighed a sigh of relief.

"What kind of business do you do with this guy and who is this partner of yours?" Chief Thompson asked, as he walked close to Freedom.

Freedom looked on nervously and stated, "We do heisting and his nickname is Havoc."

"Havoc!" Detective Long exclaimed. He looked on then thought to himself, *This can't be my Big H from Brooklyn. I know he didn't slip up like this.*

He was brought back from the thought when Freedom said, "Yes, Havoc. He killed him in cold blood. He also killed another person." He swallowed then took a deep breath and continued. "Actually, two other people, *in Connecticut.*"

Chief Thompson looked around the room, sat down, then glanced at Detective Long. He watched Freedom then said, "I think you just hit a home run." He continued, "So where is this Havoc at now?"

"He's waiting on me so that we can do another heist in a few days," Freedom said.

Detective Long looked on and thought, *If this kid knows where the heist is, Havoc and I could be in a world of trouble.* He looked at Freedom then asked, "Do you know where the heist is?" He stood up directly in front of Freedom and waited patiently for his response.

"No, sir, he didn't tell me. He usually just comes and picks me up," Freedom stated. He relaxed in the hard wooden chair.

"So, if we put you back on the street, we might nab him *and* put *this* murder on him," Mr. Hill suggested.

"Well, you got the power to do what you want."

Chief Thompson chuckled then got up and proceeded to walk out of the office. Before he left, he stated, "Long, Smith, get on it."

"Son, you did good work," Mr. Hill patted Freedom on the back then exited the office.

"We'll get this approved from our boss and then we'll put you back on the streets later," Smith stated. He gave Freedom a smile then walked out together with Long.

"So, how did it go?" Freedom asked his attorney.

"Fantastic. You hit a home run. Whenever a homicide is involved, it brings music to their ears," Mr. Holms assured. Then he motioned for the uniformed officer to place Freedom back inside the holding cell.

The officer escorted Freedom back to the cold cell and placed him inside. Freedom noticed that B.G. wasn't there. He looked at the officer and asked, "Where is Mr. Ward?"

"Oh, he bonded out and said to hold your head," the officer stated. He then closed the steel door.

Freedom dozed off for hours and was suddenly awakened by the sound of keys. When the officer opened the door, he yelled, "Lewis, get up. You have to meet with the detectives." He then guided Freedom to the R&D area and placed him in the custody of Detective Reid and Detective Jackson. The two detectives looked Freedom up and down. Reid gave Freedom some release papers to fill out while Jackson squatted down to place the house arrest bracelet around Freedom's leg.

"So I'm good now until I go to court?" Freedom asked. He was excited.

"Oh, no, Champ. You have to show us your residence and then we hook this box up to your phone. But here's the good part. You can stay out until you set your buddy up, the guy who killed someone in *my* neighborhood," Reid explained.

"Set him up?" Freedom sounded confused as he adjusted the bracelet.

"Yeah, you guys are doing a heist together, right?" Detective Reid stated then looked at Freedom with one eyebrow raised. He continued, "So you act as if you never got arrested, then you go through with the heist and get your sentence reduced.

"Ah-ight," Freedom looked on as if he knew he had his work cut out for him.

Chapter 22

Long drove down the Westside Highway until he reached the peer. He looked all over to see if he saw Havoc's car. He didn't see or hear a peep from Havoc. He glanced at his watch to check the time. His watch read 7:57. He cut his car engine off and waited on Havoc. Detective Long was startled by Havoc who knocked on his car window. The detective opened the passenger's side door. Havoc got inside, closed the door and looked at his longtime partner. He sensed something was wrong so he asked, "What's going on?"

"*What's going on?*" Detective Long shouted looking at Havoc. "I'll tell you what's wrong. It's this kid down at the station spilling his fucking guts out about how *you* killed some kid for him and how *you* two are about to do a heist together."

"What?" Havoc looked confused. He thought to himself out loud then yelled, "Don't tell me Freedom."

"Yes, *Freedom.* He got my boss and some other detectives trying to set you up." He stared at Havoc then continued. "Do you know this could lead back to me and we *both* will be in a shit load of trouble?"

"Damn, what happened?" Havoc asked. He lit up a cigar, inhaled, then blew the smoke out through his mouth and nose.

"We made a bust on 126th Street and he was there. We also have been watching him for weeks. Now my boss is in on it, so it'll be hard to cover this up," Detective Long explained. He pulled out his pad and showed Havoc the notes he took from his meeting with Freedom.

"Damn, I told that nigga to leave that crack alone," Havoc said. He took another pull off the cigar. As he blew smoke through his nose he asked, "So what do we do now?"

"Look, Big H, how many other people know what's going on besides Freedom?" Detective Long asked. He then placed his index finger on his temple.

"Just you, me, um, um," Havoc hesitated as he thought. When he remembered, he continued, "You, me, Freedom and Tommy."

"*Who the fuck is Tommy?*" Long asked as he massaged his head.

"Tommy is the bank investor that turned me on to this heist," Havoc explained. He sat back on the passenger's side and made himself comfortable. He then added, "I mean, it's five million dollars in it for me, so this heist still has to take place."

"So you better think about how you're going to dodge the feds and pull off the heist at the same time," Long assured the feds were already on to him.

"Listen, Long, this is a major lick. If I pull this off, I can leave the country if I wanted to," Havoc said. He placed the big cigar inside of the ashtray.

"This is a very interesting situation *and* dangerous," Long stated. He looked at his friend, locked eyes and said, "I'm in."

"Yo, Big L, I told you I had bad vibes about this heist," Havoc said. He pulled from his waistband a Glock 40. semi-automatic handgun and released the clip to show Long he was ready for whatever came his way.

"I don't have a clue on what will happen or how we're going to pull this off, but two-and-a-half million sounds lovely," Detective Long stated.

"So listen, this is how we'll get rid of the bank investor." Havoc watched his old partner to make sure he paid full attention, then continued. "He does a lot of white collar crimes with the people's money that invest in his bank. So you can nab him on some fraud shit and place him in Federal custody. Just until the heist is over."

"Um, hm, *very interesting*," Long thought.

"I have paperwork as we speak back at the construction company." Havoc assured his plan would work.

"Yeah, I know this hungry police officer waiting on a big break and ready to make detective," Long stated with confidence. He placed the car in drive then added, "Let's go get these papers."

"That's what I'm talking about," Havoc complemented him, then relit his cigar.

"How many days until the heist?" Long asked as he weaved in and out of traffic on his way to Brooklyn.

"Two more days and everything should be a go. The owner of the house will be on vacation," Havoc said then continued to smoke on the Perfecto cigar.

The two men arrived at the construction site. Havoc entered the building, proceeded to the office, rambled through his desk, came up with the false documents, then exited the building. He got back inside the car and showed Detective Long the paperwork. He said, "This is how he's stealing money."

"Damn, this ma fucka is very smart." Detective Long admired the bank investor's brilliant plan. He drove away slowly from the construction site. The two proceeded to go back to Manhattan. Once the duo arrived at the pier, Havoc looked at his buddy and said, "Tomorrow, same place, same time."

"Wait, you have to stay low. I'm sure they're out looking for you as we speak," Long assured. Then he made the peace sign with his index and middle fingers. Before Havoc could close the passenger side door, Long added, "If Freedom calls you, remember, you don't know what's going on, so act the same."

"Ah-ight," Havoc agreed. He then closed the door and walked across the parking lot toward his vehicle. Havoc opened the car door then got inside. He closed the door, started the engine, picked up his cell and gave Pam a call.

Ring. Ring.

"Hello," Pam answered.

"So, what's up for tonight?" Havoc asked.

"If you're not too busy, stop by," Pam said as she sat in a hot tub of water.

"Give me an hour," Havoc stated, then pulled out and got on the crowded freeway.

Chapter 23

*F*reedom and the two detectives arrived in front of his apartment building. The three men exited the car, walked through the building's doors and proceeded to Freedom's apartment. They entered the well-furnished crib and Detective Reid began searching for a place to put the house arrest monitor. Freedom guided Detective Reid up to his cozy little room where he had his own personal line. He didn't want his mother to know that he was on house arrest.

"So, this is your room," Detective Reid said as he hooked the phone wires up to the box.

"Yes, sir," Freedom answered. He paced back and forth to and from the window.

"Relax, kid, you're making me nervous," Detective Reid joked. He placed a call so he could set the range on the box.

"Oh, here's where you two went," Jackson stated, as he proceeded through the bedroom's door.

Freedom watched nervously. He thought to himself, *I hope they don't look in my closet and notice my safe.* He was brought back from his thought when Jackson began explaining the do's and don'ts.

"Don't tell anyone what you are doing and be in the house

by 8:30 p.m. until the raid," Jackson explained. He locked eyes with Freedom then continued, "So if there's any problems, here's my card." He gave Freedom a business card. The two detectives exited the apartment building, got inside the limo tinted Toyota Camry and pulled off.

Freedom intently watched the duo from his bedroom window. He witnessed the dark blue Camry creep up the avenue. Then Freedom proceeded to his stash spot. He opened his safe and noticed nothing was missing. He thought to himself, *B.G. must not have given Mercedes my message.* He picked up his house phone and gave Havoc a call.

Ring. Ring. Ring.

"What's good?" Havoc answered. He adjusted the headset to his cell phone so he could talk and concentrate on driving at the same time.

"What's poppin'?" Freedom asked. He sat on the edge of his bed and counted his stacks silently. Then before Havoc could answer, he added, "Where you at?"

"Oh, I'm out in B.K." Havoc tried not to give himself away. He gripped the steering wheel to hold the big body Benz steady.

"So what's good with the big jump off?" Freedom asked. He placed his last stack back inside his safe, then closed it.

"I'm working on it now, but I'll let you know in the morning," Havoc assured the heist was still on. He crept up Pam's block, then he searched for a parking spot.

"Ah-ight," Freedom said, then laid his head on his pillow.

"Just be in place," Havoc murmured. He hung up the call, parked his car, exited and proceeded to Pam's building. He dialed her apartment number on the pager, then waited until she buzzed him in. Pam buzzed the lock. Havoc walked through the doors, proceeded to her apartment and knocked gently on the door.

"I'm coming," Pam yelled as she trotted toward the door.

"Damn, girl," Havoc admired Pam's figure.

"Come in," Pam waved Havoc inside with her hand. She proceeded back to the living room then she said, "Lock the door behind you."

"You look just as good as the first time we met," Havoc said. He sat down beside her on the loveseat, gazed at her thick chocolate thighs and asked, "Did you put on some weight?"

"No. I've always been this size," Pam responded as she stretched her leg out so he could see that she didn't gain any weight.

"You must know that every time I'm around you my shit gets brick hard," Havoc schemed. He caressed Pam's thighs with his index and middle fingers, moved up to her pubic area, and twisted some of it. Havoc slid two fingers inside of her wet, tight pussy.

"Um, um, oh!" Pam moaned as she propped her feet up on the sofa and laid back.

"You like that?" Havoc asked. He searched for her G spot, then nibbled on her earlobe.

"Let me suck it," Pam stated. She pulled his rock hard dick out and trimmed the tip of it with her tongue. Pam massaged his meat up and down, then put it inside of her mouth. Havoc fucked Pam's mouth with long slow strokes until he filled Pam's mouth with cum. Pam looked up at him with her puppy dog eyes and said, "Damn, that was quick." She wasn't necessarily upset that he came quickly. It just took her by surprise because the last time they fucked, Havoc punished her for like an hour.

"I haven't seen you in two weeks," Havoc said, explaining why he was a five-minute man.

"Let me get on top so I can get my shit off," Pam suggested

as she climbed on top of Havoc and placed his penis inside of her. She bounced up and down. Havoc tried to control her. He gripped her waist and ass, but she rode him like a raging bull. Pam moaned as she rocked back and forth. "I'm cumming, baby." She flopped all her weight on his chest. She shook as cum came out all over his stomach, then she suggested, "Let's take a hot shower."

"Ah-ight," Havoc agreed as he struggled to get her off of him.

They went to take a shower. After their shower, they cuddled up in Pam's huge king size bed. After a while, the couple fell asleep.

Havoc was awakened by the sun that beamed through the blinds. He checked his watch for the time and thought to himself, *Tommy should be out of my way soon.* Havoc was brought back from his thought when he felt his cell phone vibrate.

"Hello," Havoc answered. He got up out of bed.

"Hey, how are you doing? We got the warrant for your friend," Detective Long assured that everything was going as planned. "Remember, stay low," Long reminded Havoc.

"Same place, same time," Havoc said as he put his clothes back on, then ended the call.

"What's wrong?" Pam asked. She lay in bed with her silk sheets over her.

"I have something to take care of," Havoc kissed her on the forehead, then exited her apartment and was off back to Brooklyn.

Chapter 24

Freedom paced around his apartment as he brushed his teeth. He thought to himself, *This nigga hasn't called me yet and I have to warn Mercedes not to come over here.* After his trip to the moon, Freedom came back to earth and called B.G.'s mother's house out in Long Island.

Ring. Ring.

"Hello," answered B.G.'s mother.

"Hi, may I speak to B.G.?" Freedom asked, with toothpaste in his mouth B.G. was nearby so his mom handed him the phone.

"What's popping?" B.G. answered. He cleared his throat and took a long stretch.

"Yo, B.G. I'm out, but listen, don't call Mercedes. I'm good," Freedom said then rinsed his mouth out with water.

"How did you get out?" B.G. wondered.

"I'll explain later," Freedom assured B.G. that he would tell him about what happened, then hung up the call.

Freedom got dressed and peeked out his window. He didn't see any F.B.I. agents so he thought to himself, *I gots to tell Havoc what happened. If it wasn't for him, I'd still be broke.* So when he returned from his trip this time, he decided to call his partner in crime, Havoc.

Ring. Ring.

"What's up, Free?" Havoc answered. He noticed the number Freedom was calling from.

"Yo, kid, I need to get at you without these phones," Freedom stated. He exited his apartment and crept inside his car.

"What's up, Free?" Havoc could sense his buddy was trying to tell him what happened, then he added, "I'll get at you in an hour. I'll be a little closer to you then."

"Yo, kid, this is important, but I don't have too much time," Freedom murmured, as he pulled off in his 745i BMW.

"In an hour," Havoc assured he would return the call, then hung up.

Havoc searched through his programmed numbers on his Nextel phone, then speed dialed Detective Long's number.

Ring. Ring.

"Hello," Long answered in his famous country tone of voice.

"Yo, where you at?" Havoc asked as he raced down the expressway.

"I'm at the station," Long stated, as he smacked on some cold ham sandwiches then he added, "Why?"

"This nigga just called me. He said he wanted to meet with me," Havoc sounded nervous.

"What did you say?" Detective Long asked. As he saw Reid and Jackson coming his way, he added, "Yo, I have to go."

"Wait a minute," Havoc yelled, then pulled his head set out and began hooking it up to his cell phone. He asked, "What should I do?"

"Go ahead. It should be safe. The detectives that are assigned to him are with me now," Detective Long let Havoc know that he wouldn't get caught up, then he ended the call.

Havoc drove back to Brooklyn to the construction site. He parked and thought, *Damn, what's this dude up to? Should I trust him and Long. Damn, Long never steered me wrong before.* He got out of his car, entered the building then proceeded to his personal office. He checked his messages and one message interested him.

"Yo, you fucking prick. You set me up. You were the only one who knew about what I was doing. You'll pay for this."

Havoc pressed off on his answering machine and smiled. Then thought to himself, *They must have his ass locked up,* then he continued out loud, "Yes."

Havoc sat at his office desk going over a few contracts that his company had coming up in a few weeks. Then his cell phone chirped.

"Hello," Havoc answered. He placed his pen down and relaxed all the way back in the comfortable office chair.

"I had to go. I'm sorry about that, but I don't want them catching feelings," Detective Long enunciated. Then he continued, "They're in the office. The kid isn't being watched so maybe he wants to tell you what happened."

"Maybe," Havoc sounded confused as he stared into space, then picked his ink pen up and placed it inside of his mouth.

"Listen, don't be nervous. I've never steered you wrong," Long assured. He paced back up the crowded precinct then continued. "I got my eye on the detectives. Trust me, he's on his own out there, so meet with him."

"Ah-ight," Havoc reluctantly agreed, then hung up his cell. He proceeded back to Harlem to meet with his partner in crime, Freedom. He dodged and weaved down the freeway and arrived on 125th Street and Broadway. He parked, got out and used a pay phone to call Freedom.

Ring. Ring.

"Yeah," answered Freedom.

"Where are you?" Havoc asked. He watched the traffic thoroughly.

"I'm around," Freedom assured he was waiting on Havoc's call, then added, "Where are you?"

"Meet me at McDonald's on 1-2-5 and Broadway. I'll be having brunch," Havoc stated then hung up the call. He dashed back to his car, got in and sat low on the driver's side. Havoc carefully peeped the entire area out. He didn't see any police, then he decided to head for McDonald's. He exited his car then hit the automatic lock button to lock all the doors. Havoc jogged across the crowded street, entered McDonald's, ordered his brunch and sat in a booth that was positioned away from the window. He checked his watch for the time and looked around. He noticed Freedom standing in the lobby area.

"Yo, I'm over here," Havoc waved Freedom over with his hand.

"What's good?" Freedom asked as he sat down in the booth, then continued, "Sorry I'm late."

"What's so important?" Havoc asked. He locked eyes with his partner, then reached for his gun that he had tucked in his waistband.

"Yo, um, um, yo, man," Freedom stuttered then he looked his friend in the eye, and continued. "Yo, man, I got knocked yesterday."

"What do you mean you got knocked?" Havoc asked, then pulled his semi-automatic handgun out and placed the barrel on Freedom's knee under the table.

"Yo, man, I had to get out, so listen, man, I told them you killed Trey. I didn't tell them your government though," Freedom was crying. He wiped his face so no one could witness his tears.

"You told them what?" Havoc yelled then cocked his hammer. "I should put a hot one in you right now."

"No, please, don't kill me, please. I'm sorry, but I had to warn you. I'm about to bounce out of the state. I just got my passport," Freedom begged then reached in his pocket to show Havoc his fake passport. Then added, "I just thought if I came to you before they did, you could get away somehow."

"Why you had to say *me*?" Havoc asked. He looked at Freedom with the devil in his eye.

"I know I fucked up. I told them you got a job in a couple of days, so they want me to set you up," Freedom explained, trembling.

"So listen. I'll get out of this mess if you keep them away," Havoc said as he uncocked his gun and placed it back in his waistband. "So meet me back here at 10 o'clock."

Freedom interrupted. "Wait, they got me on house arrest," Freedom pulled up his pant leg to show Havoc his bracelet, then added, "I gots to be in by 8:30."

"Check this out. In the morning I'll call you and let you know what to do," Havoc watched Freedom close then continued. "So don't fuck this up or I'll kill you." Havoc stood up from the table and walked away. He jogged back across the street, got inside his car and drove away. On his way back to Brooklyn, he called an old friend named Doe.

Ring. Ring. Ring.

"Speak to me," Doe answered.

"Yo, what's good?" Havoc asked as he concentrated on the freeway.

"Who is this, Havoc?" Doe asked as he blew smoke out of his nose.

"Yeah, this is Havoc," Havoc stated.

"What's up, playboy?" Doe asked.

"I got a business deal for you," Havoc sounded excited as he sat low in his Mercedes.

"What kind of deal?" Doe asked.

"Meet me at Prospect Park in twenty minutes," Havoc demanded, then ended the call.

Doe was an old school drug dealer that controlled most of the heroin that came into Flatbush, Brooklyn, and if he could make any side deals, he was in. Two years ago, Havoc and Doe had a run in. Havoc had schemed on one of Doe's locations, but when Havoc made his move on the heist, he learned that the spot belonged to Doe. All over the Flatbush area, Doe had soldiers working for him. So Doe got wind that Havoc was scheming on his riches. He had a couple of his soldiers kidnap Havoc and bring him in. Once he was brought in, Doe asked him, "Who you working for?"

"I'm not working for anyone," Havoc wouldn't give his connects that easy.

"If he doesn't want to talk, put a bullet in his head," Doe demanded his soldiers. One of the soldiers pointed his gun at Havoc's head, pulled the trigger, but his gun jammed. After Havoc realized that Doe was serious, he agreed to tell him. "Spike, he gave me the run down."

"Okay, you must be lucky. My man's gun never jammed," Doe assured that he was going to kill him.

"I told Spike if I knew it was *your* spot, I wouldn't have agreed," Havoc lied, as his gums bumped together.

"So you set Spike up for me and I'll pay you seventy-five thousand dollars," Doe yelled. He looked at Havoc in the eye then added, "If you don't do it, I'll have my men kill you."

"I'll do it," Havoc agreed. He walked out of Doe's spot and went to find Spike. He continued to go along with Spike's plan to hit Doe's stash spot for twenty bricks of heroin, but when he got there, Doe and his soldiers were in place. They killed Spike by putting two bullets in his head and just like Doe said, he paid Havoc seventy-five thousand dollars and told him never to try that again and if he wanted, he would put Havoc on his payroll. Havoc declined, but said if he ever knew if someone was plotting on his stash houses, he would let him know, and if he could ever do any business with him, he would.

Havoc arrived at the park in exactly fifteen minutes, parked, exited his car and searched around for Doe.

"I'm over here," Doe yelled, then waved to Havoc with his hand. Doe was in the cut with two broads. But his henchmen were posted up on Front Street letting whoever know that it wasn't going down.

"How you doing?" Havoc asked as the two men walked through the park.

"So, what's going on?" Doe asked. He looked at Havoc, then reached out to shake his hand. "I know this must be big if you're calling me."

"Yeah, it's big, and I need some power," Havoc explained then he added, "It's worth five million dollars. We can split it two and a half a piece."

"I'm in," Doe agreed with a firm handshake.

"Well, the location is out in Jersey City." Havoc explained every detail of the location and the two men departed and went their separate ways.

Havoc got back inside of his car and thought to himself, *If I know Doe like I think I do, he'll try and double cross me on this heist.* When Havoc returned from his space mission, he was in front of the construction company. He exited the car, entered the building and checked his files. He noticed on the file that the house in Jersey City was finished. All the garbage and debris had been removed. Once he went back on his mission to space, he thought, *This is perfect.* He was startled by his cell phone vibrating on the desk.

Ring. Ring.

"Hello," Havoc answered.

"Where you at?" Detective Long asked.

"I'm at the site," Havoc said, then pulled his office chair up and took a seat. "Why?" he asked.

"Because the agents just left to go meet your man," Long wanted Havoc to get low if he wasn't already.

"I already met with him," Havoc stated.

"So have you decided how we're going to get those diamonds?" Long asked. He exited the precinct and got into his car.

"We'll talk in person," Havoc reminded Long that they would still be meeting at the pier.

"Alright," Detective Long agreed. He put his car into drive and drove off. As he followed behind the other detectives to meet with Freedom, he said, "I'll be there," then hung up the call.

Chapter 25

Meanwhile, in Flatbush, Brooklyn... Doe and a few of his most loyal soldiers geared up to pay the house out in Jersey City a visit to make sure Havoc was telling him the truth. The team of men raced down the freeway back to back in two black Suburbans. They arrived in front of the house and watched the location through the dark tinted truck windows.

"Everything looks good," Doe said as he pulled out a pair of binoculars to get a closer view of the back entrance of the house. He then continued, "If this kid isn't lying, we can do this tomorrow night, without him."

"Yeah, that nigga owes you for saving his life," one of the soldiers commented.

"Tomorrow night we'll make a move on it. It should be five million dollars worth of diamonds in there," Doe explained every detail to his notorious gang. Then added, "Let's get out of here."

Back at Freedom's apartment...

Freedom parked, got out of his car and jogged through the security doors. He raced up the staircase to his apartment, entered his pad and proceeded to his bedroom. He glanced at his watch and thought to himself, *It's getting late. I have to put this passport in a safe place.* He came back from his thoughts when he heard someone knocking at his door. He opened his safe, put the document in it and closed it back up. Then he answered the door.

Knock. Knock.

"Who is it?" Freedom yelled as he looked through his peep-hole.

"It's the F.B.I.," Long joked as he caught up with the others.

"Come in. I wasn't expecting you guys this early." Freedom opened the door and looked at his watch to check the time.

"It's 7 o'clock. You should be ending your day anyways," Detective Reid joked as he and his partners entered the two-bedroom apartment. He continued, "Well, the chief sent us to ask you a few questions."

"What's up?" Freedom asked. The look on his face was a confused one.

"Well, is this guy dangerous?" Long asked as he closed the door and continued to walk where the others stood.

"I mean, shit, he murdered a *few* of people," Freedom enunciated. He offered the agents a seat with a simple wave of the hand.

"So do you have his cell number?" Detective Smith asked, as he pulled out his pad and jotted down notes.

Freedom's eyes widened. He watched the officers then he responded, "Um, um, it's 646-um, 5-4-8-4."

"Good. Good," Smith congratulated Freedom with a pat on the back.

"There's no certain time, but tomorrow at..." Before he finished his sentence, he watched the detectives and Detective Long's eyes got big as golf balls as he waited for Freedom to cross Havoc. Then Freedom continued, "...around 12 noon."

"Twelve noon, so we'll stay close by," Jackson suggested. Detective Long traveled to outer space and thought, *I have to warn Havoc.* When he came back to earth, he noticed it was almost 8 o'clock. Then he said, "I have to end this guys. I have a date with the old lady, so we'll have to continue this tomorrow at noon."

Detective Long exited the apartment, jumped in his compact Toyota and proceeded to the pier. He dipped in and out of traffic until he reached the Westside Highway, then continued to blow down the crowded freeway toward the pier.

"So, Freedom, we'll see you tomorrow around noonish," Detective Smith assured as the remaining two Detectives left Freedom's apartment, then he added, "Tomorrow *is* the dead line."

"I know, I know," Freedom said as he stood in the doorway. Then he added, "I hope this goes well," with the thought of leaving the country in mind, then he closed the door.

Havoc raced down the Westside Highway on his way to the pier. When he got there, he searched for a spot to park. He noticed Detective Long's headlights. Havoc parked, dashed over to Long's small Toyota Camry, got inside, and adjusted the passenger's side seat.

"How's it going?" Detective Long asked as he cut the engine off."

"I'm ah-ight," Havoc greeted Long with a hand shake, then continued, "How are you?"

"Well, we just had a meeting with Freedom, and he said you were dangerous, plus he said you were meeting him tomorrow at noon," Long explained as he watched the cars pass by.

"Good. I told him in the morning so he must be trying to buy some time," Havoc sighed a sigh of relief, then continued, "I'm going to send Freedom and an old friend of mines to

Jersey City, while you and I will be out in Alpine, New Jersey. So, after you make that bust, Free'll tell them that my friend is me and you'll meet me at the mansion I showed you."

"So you got somebody to take the weight for you?" Long asked. He looked surprised.

"Don't worry, this dude thinks it's diamonds at the address out in Jersey City, so me knowing him, five million dollars worth of diamonds will make him double cross me," Havoc explained, as he propped his foot up on the dashboard. Then he added, "I need your help though."

"I know, I know," Detective Long said as he looked on. "So will this guy go down easy?" he asked.

"Oh, no, he's one of the biggest kingpins in the city, so you'll get a two for one deal," Havoc assured that he would need back up.

"I guess I'm in," Long reluctantly agreed.

"You should be okay. Just remember, stay low and keep firing," Havoc advised his partner on how to make it out alive. He exited the car. Before he closed the door he said, "Remember, wear your vest," Havoc closed the door and disappeared into the night.

Back at Freedom's apartment...

Freedom picked up his cell phone and dialed Mercedes' number.

Ring. Ring.

"Hello," Mercedes answered.

"What's up, baby?" Freedom asked as he sat on the edge of his bed with a blank look on his face. "Yo, listen to me. I got something to take care of tomorrow, so like I said before, if you don't hear from me in a couple of days, give my mother the number." Freedom couldn't tell her that he was about to leave the country.

"Ah-ight, but why are you doing it if you know it's a chance you might get killed?" Mercedes cried.

"I have to, baby, but remember, I love you," Freedom comforted her then ended the call.

Chapter 26

*T*he next morning around 8 o'clock, Havoc pulled up to 1-2-5 and Broadway, exited his rental car and placed a call to Freedom on the pay phone.

Ring. Ring. Ring.

"What's up?" Freedom answered. He took a long stretch.

"You're not up?" Havoc asked as he kept a look out for any strange cars.

"Where are you?" Freedom asked. He got up and searched for his keys.

"I'm in the same spot as yesterday," Havoc stated, then hung up the pay phone. He crossed the busy street, then entered inside of McDonald's and sat in the exact same booth. He waited for Freedom. Twenty minutes passed, and Freedom trotted down the sidewalk, entered the restaurant and searched for his man. Once he spotted him, he dashed to the booth and took a seat on the opposite side directly in front of Havoc. The two locked eyes for a half a second then Havoc asked, "No one followed you, right?"

"We good. I bought myself a few hours," Freedom assured his buddy that they were safe.

"Here's the plan. I told this kid from B.K. about the heist, so he's going to be there. All you have to do is..." Havoc paused, looked around to see if anyone was listening, then he contin- ued. "...All you have to do is tell them he's me. You get your time cut, still have your money, and the Feds will pin him with the bodies."

"Okay," Freedom agreed. He looked at his partner and con- tinued, "This could work out."

"Yo, if you do what you're supposed to do, it'll work," Havoc stated. He watched Freedom, then he continued, "Yo, Free, don't fuck me or you *will* die."

Freedom looked around the crowded restaurant and he sensed that his partner in crime was serious, then he stated, "Yo, don't worry. I got you." He gave Havoc a quick head nod.

"I hope so, because I'm not trying to go to jail," Havoc assured he was not spending a day locked up.

"So, when I get there, this kid will be there, then I tell them that it's you? And what will be in the house?" Freedom went back over every detail as he looked at his partner.

"Yes, just tell them I'm in the house and that I didn't tell you I was going to be there. Tell them I acted like I knew some- thing," Havoc explained his brilliant plan. Then he got up and proceeded to walk off. He turned around and added, "Remember, stay low and you'll make it out alive." Then he walked out, got into his rental car and drove off. As he drove, he thought to himself, *It's going to be a lot of blood shed if this works. I hope these ma fuckas stay low and make it out, or I'm going to have war on my hands with Doe and the Feds.* When Havoc returned from his thought, he arrived at his construction site in Brooklyn. He tried to call Doe on his cell phone but got no answer. He got out of his car, walked through the door of the company's office, placed his car keys on the desk, took a seat, crossed his legs and returned back to Mars to figure out a plan.

I hope Doe hasn't figured out my plan. When he came back to civilization, he called Long.

Ring. Ring. Ring.

"Hello," Long answered as he put on his vest, loaded his semi-automatic handgun and tucked it inside of his holster.

"What's good, Big L?" Havoc asked as he rested his head on the desk.

"We're about to go meet my boss then set up shop around your boy, Freedom," Detective Long responded as he put his favorite police jacket on.

"So, 9 o'clock, everything should pop off. I told the kid 10:30, so I know he'll try and make it there earlier than me," Havoc explained.

"I'll try and convince these dudes to go around 8:30," Long stated. Then he proceeded down the hallway where the others were.

"Around 11 o'clock, meet me out in Alpine. I'll be there with the diamonds, so don't be late," Havoc raised his head off of the desk and continued, "And don't double cross me."

"I should be worried about *you*. *You're* the one with all the *planning*," Long reminded Havoc that *he* was the one in the situation. Then ended the call.

Doe and his posse got ready for the heist. They all met at a secret stash house out on Long Island where they gathered all types of guns and ammo.

"Hey, you got the double barrel pump with the pistol grip?" one of Doe's soldiers asked as he searched through the basement of the house.

"Yeah, over there," Doe said as he pointed to his special double barrel pump. He held the gun up in the air. "This gun has a lot of bodies on it." He looked at it, admiring it for its power.

"And a lot more to come," the soldier laughed as he grabbed the shotgun.

"So, this ho ass nigga said he was going out there around 10 o'clock, so we'll go a couple of hours earlier, and if anybody's home, we'll kill everything moving," Doe ordered his gang.

"Nine o'clock it is," the soldiers cheered as they all cocked their guns.

The detectives all arrived at Freedom's apartment. They called Freedom on the phone.

Ring. Ring.

"Hello," Freedom answered as he looked out his window, then looked at his mother.

"We're coming in," Jackson demanded as he parked the old Buick.

"No, wait, I'm coming out," Freedom kissed his mother, gave her a hug, exited the apartment and got inside of the car with the other detectives.

"How is it going, kid?" Long asked. He turned around and looked at Freedom in the back seat.

"I'm ah-ight," Freedom answered as he got comfortable in the cramped back seat of the Buick.

"When is it going down?" Smith asked as he placed his arm around the back of Freedom's neck.

"Well, I spoke to him this morning and he said he wasn't doing it tonight, but he sounded like he knew something was up," Freedom explained. He watched the detectives to see if they bought his story. Then he added, "But I know the address and I think he's doing it once it gets dark."

Smith watched all of his partners, then locked eyes with Freedom. He raised his eyebrow and stated, "I hope you're not lying to us, kid."

"Oh, no, I'm not pulling your leg," Freedom tried to cover up his nervousness.

"So we'll go see if he's doing it tonight around 9 o'clock," Long suggested. He smiled because he knew Havoc's plan was falling into place. Then he said, "So, kid, we'll be back here around 8 o'clock to get you so you can show us the place."

"Ah-ight," Freedom agreed. He looked at his fellow men then closed his eyes as if to say, *Thank you, Jesus.* He exited the car and proceeded to *his* car.

"Do you think we should follow him?" Smith asked as he watched Freedom get inside his vehicle.

"No, I believe the kid. He's scared to death," Long stated, then looked at his partner with reassurance.

Havoc exited the building, jumped inside of his rental car and headed for Jersey City to make sure that his plan was in order. As he traveled down the freeway, he watched the traffic through his rearview mirror consistently. He arrived at the location, parked, got out then proceeded to the house. He looked through the windows and entered the house. He thought to himself, *This is perfect. I can pull this off.* He came back from his thought when he noticed that the basement door was open. He smiled and thought, *Someone has been here. Doe.* Havoc reached inside his pocket, pulled out a purple Crown Royal bag that contained an undetermined amount of cocaine, placed it in a spot in the basement, then stared into space and thought, *If they kill anybody, it will be drug related and Doe will be behind bars forever.* When he came back from this thought, he entered his car and drove back to New York.

Chapter 27

Freedom waited for the detectives to arrive back at his place. He checked his Frank Mueller watch for the time. It read 8:02. He thought to himself, *Maybe they knew I was lying and they're going to try and lock me back up.* He snapped out of his daydream when he noticed two unmarked cars traveling up his block. Freedom stood up to get a better view of the vehicle. The unmarked Toyotas stopped directly in front of Freedom's stoop. Reid rolled down his window and motioned for Freedom to get in. Freedom got in the back and stated, "Long time no hear from."

"Listen, kid, cut the jokes," Jackson said as he looked in the back seat, then added, "Tell us where this friend of yours might be."

"Okay, get on the freeway and hit the Holland Tunnel," Freedom explained as he raised up and peeked out the back window. Then he asked, "Is that the other detectives?"

"Yeah," Reid answered as he concentrated on the road.

Meanwhile, Doe and his gang arrived at the location down in Jersey City. They parked, got out and proceeded through the basement entrance. The notorious gang searched up and down the half finished house. Doe ordered, "You, go to the front entrance and keep a lookout for anything funny." He looked at his soldier and continued, "If you see anyone scheming, let them have it."

"Ah-ight, Boss," The soldier sounded excited as he grabbed the A.K. 47 assault rifle and headed to the front of the house.

The detectives arrived at the house. They parked and called for backup. Freedom watched the house and noticed someone standing in front of the premises. He stated, "Look, there he is," as he pointed and locked eyes with Jackson.

"Ten-four," Reid yelled through the walkie talkie then continued, "I think we are on to something."

"I read you loud and clear," Long's eyes widened as he looked at his partner.

"I called for back up but they're not here yet," Reid stated, as he pulled out his gun. "Let's see what's going on," he continued.

The detectives exited their vehicles and proceeded to the house with their guns out. Reid led the way with his semi-automatic handgun in front of him. He screamed, "Police! Freeze! Don't move!"

The lookout noticed the police and screamed, "Go fuck yourself," as he opened fire on the officers. Bullets pierced cars and houses.

"Get down. Get down," Long demanded to his partners as he fell to the ground and propped his fist under his gun and fired back.

"What the fuck is going on out there?" Doe asked as he grabbed and cocked his favorite pump. He dashed out the basement doors and noticed police lights all over the place. He paused for a second, aimed at the blue and white police cars and began firing. The other posse members followed suit and fired their guns as well.

Jackson stood up and said, "Cover me, I'm going to take him out."

"Wait a minute," Reid said as he grabbed at his partner's coat, but couldn't hold on to it.

"Die ma fucka," one of the soldiers yelled as he let off a series of shots at Jackson's head. The impact from the bullets blew his head all over the yard.

Freedom crawled out of the car and tried to make a get away up the street. From behind a tree he noticed a double barrel shotgun pointed in his direction. He got up from his position and tried to out run the bullets, but the two bullets entered through his body from his back and exited through his chest. Freedom fell to the ground and cried, "I've been shot. I've been shot." He was trembling as blood leaked from his torso.

"Call an ambulance," one of the uniformed officers yelled as they all aimed their semi-automatic handguns in Doe's direction. Doe dashed through back yards, hearing bullets ricocheting off of the surrounding houses. Doe escaped. Once he got far enough, he hid inside of someone's old garage that was filled with landscaping equipment. He stared into space and thought out loud, "I'm going to kill you, Havoc."

At the scene of the crime, several officers were killed, and some were critically wounded, including Detective Jackson. All the members of the notorious *posse* were assumed dead. Detective Long observed the dead bodies and remembered that he had to meet Havoc. He approached his partner and said, "I have a hunch that we didn't get them all. Something the kid said to me earlier when we were alone. Stay here and see what you come up with. I have to go check something."

His partner tapped him on the shoulder and said, "Long, go ahead. I'll stay here and see if they find anything." Smith looked at his partner and the look on his face said that he was tired and it was going to be a long night.

Detective Long got inside his unmarked car and proceeded to Alpine, New Jersey to meet Havoc. He looked at his watch to check the time. It was 10 o'clock. He weaved through traffic until he arrived in front of the location. He pulled his handgun out and crept inside the mansion. Long reached the basement door. It was unlocked. He peeked in and didn't see any signs of Havoc. He entered the basement and let the door close softly behind him. He searched through the basement and heard a noise coming from the outside of the house. He turned around when he heard the basement door open and noticed it was Havoc.

Havoc was startled. He pulled his gun out and said, "Damn, you scared me." Havoc lowered his gun and wiped the sweat from his brow.

"I guess I made it here before you," Long stated as he looked into Havoc's eyes.

"I got the diamonds right here. They were right underneath the basement staircase," Havoc sounded excited about his *last* heist, then he continued, "Come on, let's get the fuck out of here."

"Wait a minute," Long said as he grabbed Havoc's arm. "Freedom is dead. He didn't make it."

"Damn," Havoc lowered his head, raised it again, looked at Long's face as if he were trying to read him, pictured his old pal lying in his own blood and asked, "What happened?"

"I think one of the guys that were there got away and somehow shot him in the back," Detective Long explained as he watched Havoc closely.

"Fuck it. Let's get out of here. We got five million dollars in diamonds and we got a clean getaway," Havoc assured his plan had worked.

The duo exited the mansion and entered their cars. They agreed to drive out to the construction site to split the jewelry. Havoc led the way with Detective Long close behind him. They arrived at the site, got out of their cars and walked toward the trailer. Detective Long slowed up and let Havoc walk in front of him. He pulled out his gun, cocked it and demanded Havoc turn around. "Turn around!"

Shocked, Havoc turned around and said, "What?" His face was as pale as a dead man's. He stood with his arms out as if to say, *Why?"*

"Hand over the diamonds," Long grabbed the diamonds out of Havoc's hand and said, "I'm sorry it has to be this way."

Havoc looked around at his construction company, then locked eyes with Long and said in a defeated manner, "You know what?" he paused for a second, then continued. "I ain't mad at ya," Then he reached for his semi-automatic handgun that rested in his waistband and made an unsuccessful attempt to reverse the situation. But Detective Long's hard work and police training paid off. Long squeezed the trigger and fired two shots that entered Havoc's neck and left shoulder. Havoc fell to the ground paralyzed from the shots. He gasped for air. Detective Long walked up to his body, looked down at him and said, "Rest in peace." He gave Havoc two more to the head, looked at the diamonds, smiled and disappeared into the night.

Fan Mail Page

If you have any further questions, comments or concerns, kindly address your inquires in care of:

Travis "Unique" Stevens

At

AMIAYA ENTERTAINMENT
P.O.BOX 1275
NEW YORK, NY 10159

tanianunez79@hotmail.com

Coming Soon

From
Amiaya Entertainment LLC

"Against The Grain"
by
G. B. Johnson

&

"All Or Nothing"
by
Michael Whitby

www.amiayaentertainment.com

Flower's Bed

Flower's Bed in an incredible tale of a young lady who overcomes her adversities by experiencing pain, understanding reality and surrendering to love. At nine years old, Flower Abrams is as innocent as she was when she was first born. Cared for by both her loving mother and deceitful father, tragedy strikes this young child at an age where teddy bears and lollipops can past for best friends and lunch. Emotionally and psychologically affected by this malicious and brutal attack, flower turned to the one thing that brought her solace...the streets.

Flower's Bed

The Most Controversial Book Of This Era

Written By

Antoine "Inch" Thomas

Suspenseful...Fastpaced...Richly Textured

PUBLISHED BY AMIAYA ENTERTAINMENT

No Regrets

Anthony Wheeler is no different from thousands of poor children growing up in his Bronx housing project. He is being raised by a single mother, as are his two bests friends Dev and Slick, and life for them is as normal as it can be in a housing project under the cloud of violence, drugs and constant murders. But then Anthony goes to visit a relative one day and stumbles onto something that changes his life forever. He is intoxicated by the dreamlike lure of fast money and immediate success that the underworld and drug trafficking offers. He plunges head-on into it and spirals downward to the commission of a crime that could land him in jail for the remainder of his life. Like many of his mates, being in prison forces Anthony to have second thoughts about the path he has chosen. Once the doors clang shut behind him. But, unlike the others, instead of this revelation coming over time, Anthony's metamorphosis happens almost immediately after he is incarcerated. He says he has "No Regrets," but there is a distinctive plaintiveness in the voice echoing in his head about the path he has chosen. He seeks redemption by saying over and over to himself, "Only God can judge me."

From the Underground Bestseller "Flower's Bed"
Author Antoine "Inch" Thomas delivers you

NO REGRETS

It's Time To Get It Popping

AVAILABLE NOW FROM
AMIAYA ENTERTAINMENT
ISBN# 0-9745075-1-2

"Gritty....Realistic Conflicts....Intensely Eerie"
Published by Amiaya Entertainment

Unwilling to Suffer

Stephanie Manning is a Stunningly beautiful woman with the brains to match her incredible physical gifts. But, with all she has going for her, she has a problemshe's saddled with a husband, Darryl, who can't contain himself in the presence of other beautiful women.

Blinded by love, Stephanie at first denies there was a problem, until one day her husband's blatant infidelity catches up with him, and all hell breaks loose. The marriage crumbles, the couple separates and Stephanie files for divorce, but that's just the beginning of the madness.

Darryl finds himself caught up in more and more bizarre situations with other women while Stephanie tries her best to keep it all together. She is approached by a young thug in the 'hood and becomes engulfed in a baffling sea of emotions as she is drawn into the young man's romantic web.

Will Stephanie's and Darryl's relationship survive, or will Stephanie succumb to the young thug's advances? Find out in this enchanting and engaging story if stephanie is able to avoid being drawn into a world of sex, drama and violence.

That Gangsta Sh!t

That Gangsta Sh!t is an anthology which features "Inch", as well as several other authors. Each author will mesmerize readers as they journey through the suspense and harsh realities that are a few of the reluctant foundations of life. These shocking tales will fascinate, so much that readers won't be able to close the book.

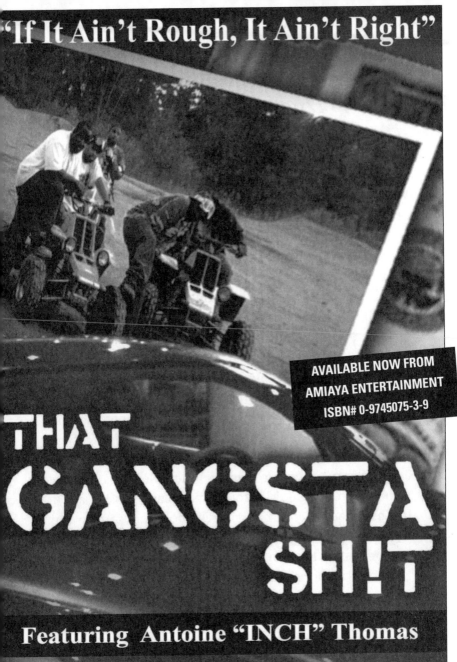

"If It Ain't Rough, It Ain't Right"

THAT GANGSTA SH!T

Featuring Antoine "INCH" Thomas

Shocking...Horrific...
You'll Be To Scared To Put It Down
Published By Amiaya Entertainment LLC

A Diamond in the Rough

A Diamond in the Rough is the compelling tale of Diamond Weatherspoon's life growing up in the ghetto neighborhoods of Brooklyn, NY. Diamond witnesses her mother Angel, who is 15 years her senior, abused and mistreated by her father Rahmel, a womanizer and major player in the lucrative crack game. When Diamond's mother finally summons up the courage to leave Rahmel, she and Diamond are forced to go on public assistance. Already abused and battered in spirit, Diamond and Angel find themselves living in a woman's shelter until the welfare system can find them adequate housing. Diamond's plans of going to college are interrupted and her dreams of a better life deferred.

Shaped by a life of pain and disappointments, Diamond turns to the Brooklyn streets for refuge. Embracing the shiesty lifestyle of the hustlers in pursuit of the easy life, Diamond encounters many types of people. When she meets Shymeek, an up and coming music producer, the dark hell she calls life begins to look brighter. Finally, Diamond has some breathing room. But things are not always what they seem. Life can change drastically at any moment. Journey into the world of Diamond Witherspoon whose story mirrors so many of our young women that are caught up in the chase for a better life. *A Diamond in the Rough* is a stark reminder that in every city neighborhood there is a rough jewel waiting to be polished to brilliance.

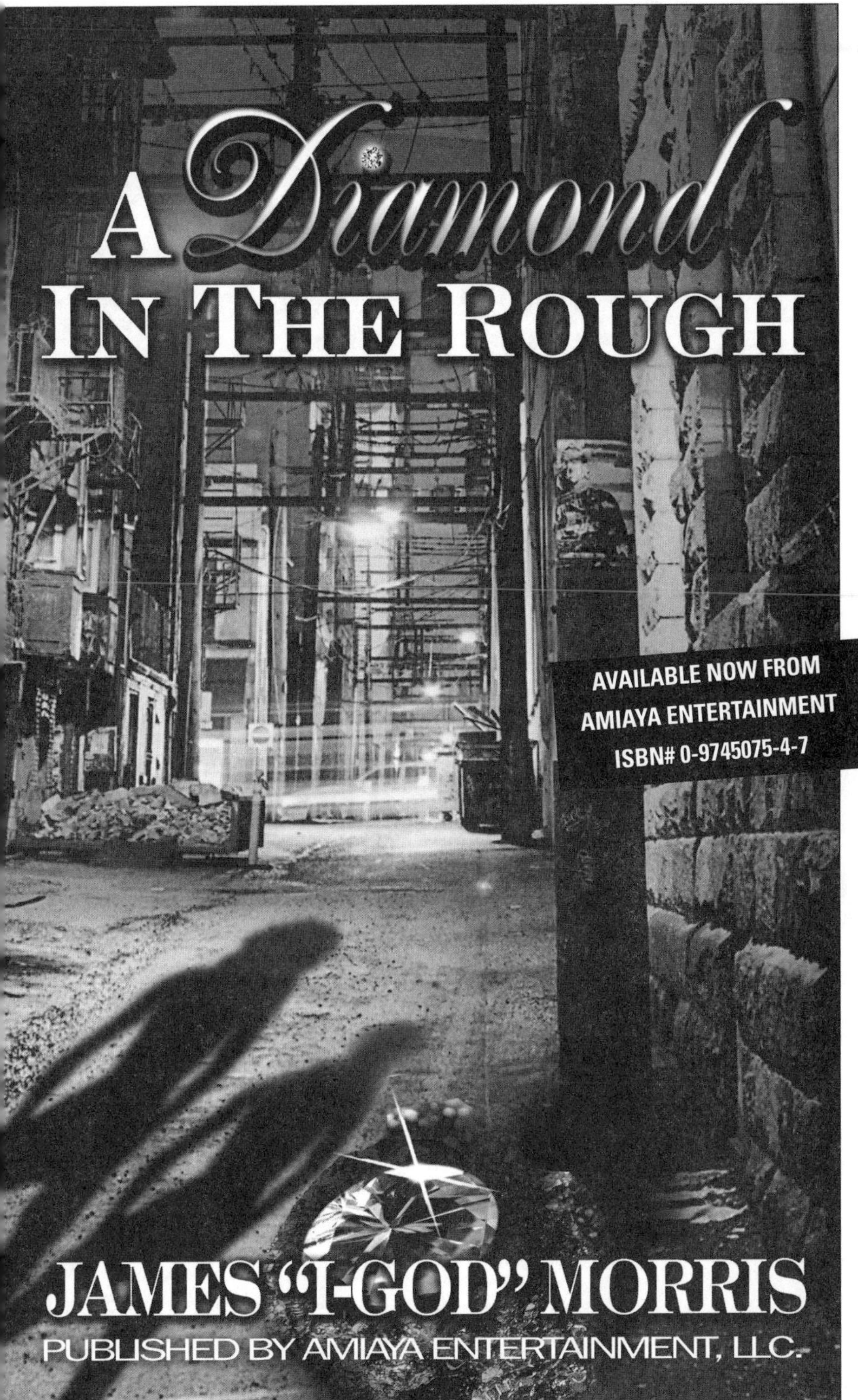
A Diamond
In The Rough
AVAILABLE NOW FROM
AMIAYA ENTERTAINMENT
ISBN# 0-9745075-4-7
JAMES 'I-GOD' MORRIS
PUBLISHED BY AMIAYA ENTERTAINMENT, LLC.

I Ain't Mad At Ya

ORDER FORM

Number of Copies

I Ain't Mad At Ya	ISBN# 0-9745075-5-5	$15.00/Copy	_____
Diamonds In The Rough	ISBN# 0-9745075-4-7	$15.00/Copy	_____
Flower's Bed	ISBN# 0-9745075-0-4	$14.95/Copy	_____
That Gangsta Sh!t	ISBN# 0-9745075-3-9	$15.00/Copy	_____
No Regrets	ISBN# 0-9745075-1-2	$15.00/Copy	_____
Unwilling To Suffer	ISBN# 0-9745075-2-0	$15.00/Copy	_____

PRIORITY POSTAGE (4-6 DAYS US MAIL): Add $4.95

Accepted form of Payments: Institutional Checks or Money Orders

(All Postal rates are subject to change.)

Please check with your local Post Office for change of rate and schedules.

Please Provide Us With Your Mailing Information:

Billing Address_____

Name: _____

Address:_____

Suite/Apartment#: _____

City:_____

Zip Code:_____

Shipping Address

Name:_____

Address:_____

Suite/Apartment#:_____

City:_____

Zip Code:_____

(Federal & State Prisoners, Please include your Inmate Registration Number)

Send Checks or Money Orders to:
AMIAYA ENTERTAINMENT
P.O.BOX 1275
NEW YORK, NY 10159
212-946-6565

www.amiayaentertainment.com

Here's an excerpt from:

Only Way Out

TRAVIS "UNIQUE" STEVENS

SOPHOMORE BOOK

Chapter 1

"We have him with us now as we speak." Ill Bill confirmed his position through the direct connect service on his Nextel cell phone.

"Bring 'em to the ave." Lex made his whereabouts known. He stared at his underboss, Rich, then gave him a sly grin as if to say, *we got 'em,* then he ended the call.

Ill Bill and the *Wide Awake Posse* traveled discretely through the streets. Within minutes they arrived at the location on Grand Avenue. The team of thugs parked outside of a five story abandoned building that was surrounded by liquor stores, bodegas, drug dealers and fiends. The notorious gang somehow managed to maneuver their victim through the building's garage door unnoticed. Once inside the large empty building, Ill Bill drew his semi-automatic handgun, then poked the victim's head with the barrel. Lex complimented his team on their excellent skills of capturing *Squirrel,* the man that owed him money. "Good, good." Lex walked toward Squirrel, looked at him up and down, then said, "So where's my 100 grand?"

"I...I...needed more time. I...I...something came up." Squirrel stuttered as he dropped to his knees and begged, "Please, don't kill me."

"Squirrel, my friend, I gave you a week already, so no more games," Lex explained to his prisoner. He looked Squirrel in the eye, frowned his face as if he were a pit bull, and before Lex could order the hit, Rich interrupted, "Let me off this nigga." Rich then pulled his chrome 44 revolver out and pointed it at Squirrel's head.

"Please, Lex, don't let him do this to me," Squirrel cried. He laid in the fetal position with his arm and hand extended to shield himself from the bullets.

"Dead that nigga," Lex ordered his lieutenant, Ill Bill, to carry out the brutal homicide. Lex then waved Rich to come with him. Before the two men exited the building, Lex turned and added, "Make sure you dismantle his body and dump his head in acid, then carry the remains to the scrap yard."

Lex and Rich left the building, got inside of Lex's luxury Range Rover. Rich started the engine, but before the two drove away, Rich looked at his boss and said, "Damn, you never let me in on the action."

"Easy, easy, you my only homie. You don't need to be getting your hands dirty," Lex convinced Rich that he didn't need to be catching any unnecessary cases. Then he continued. "Where's the T Mobile?"

"In the console." Rich pointed, without taking his eyes off of the road.

Lex lifted up the console, grabbed his T Mobile sidekick, flipped the keyboard out and typed in a text message to his girlfriend, Sahara. Sahara had an identical phone as well. Lex closed the keyboard and waited for his favorite song to play from the phone's speaker. Jay Z's *In My Life Time* was an indicator that he was receiving an incoming call. Five minutes had passed then he heard, *"In my life time, I need to see a whole lot of cash, a whole lot of,"* echoing from the phone's speaker.

"What's up?" Lex answered before his favorite song of all time could end. He adjusted the phone's earpiece so he could hear better.

"What's up, Boo?" Sahara asked.

"Where you at?" Lex questioned her as he snuggled himself low on the passenger's side.

"Where else would I be?" Sahara said in a sarcastic tone of voice. She pranced around Lex's townhouse with just a T-shirt and panties on, showing off her 5'4", 130 pound frame.

"I'm on my way so stay put," Lex told his sweetheart of nearly one year. Then he ended the call.

Lex was a slim dude in his late twenties. He stood 6'2", around 200 pounds, dark skinned, big brown eyes, jet black hair, and if you didn't know any better, you would think he was Spanish. Lex grew up in a neighborhood called *The Ville*. The Ville was known for raising drug dealers and murderers. Lex started out selling packages of heroin for a Dominican guy named Sky. The reason Sky named himself that was because to him, the *sky* was the limit.

Lex hustled on Winchester Avenue from sun up to sundown. If you wanted to locate Lex, that was where you could find him.

One day he ran into a little confrontation with a dude they called *Two Guns Up*. Two Guns Up was a short, stocky dude in his mid twenties, 5'6", 215 pounds. He had a light complexion, and if you just caught a glimpse of him, you would think you had just seen Heavy D, the rapper.

Two Guns Up controlled most of the crack throughout the entire Ville neighborhood. Although he could go on any of the neighborhood's area blocks and serve fiends, his favorite spot was at a nightclub called the Jump, Jump. The Jump, Jump was known for supplying the area with hot entertainment and beautiful women. Two Guns Up was a party animal, but first and foremost, a business man.

"He noticed" one day that most of his traffic (fiends) was going further up the avenue, towards Lex and his heroin spot. Lex's heroin was so good that it could turn a true crack head into a dope fiend, simply from word of mouth. Due to a lack of sales, Two Guns Up set out to rob his new competition, but before his plan could go underway, it was brought to his attention that Lex was a part of the infamous *Sky Cartel*. Two Guns Up decided to proposition Lex with the idea to rob Lex's connect. When Lex reluctantly agreed, after thinking it over, the two men also made a vow that if the heist went as planned, they wouldn't indulge into the other one's drug business, that Lex wouldn't sell crack, and Two Guns Up wouldn't sell heroin.

"Yo, son, I'm telling you, if we get this nigga right, we'll never have to worry about shit." Two Guns Up spoke to Lex emphasizing with hand movements.

"He supposed to have like twenty bricks of that boy tomorrow," Lex informed his new partner.

"Yo, son, I got this ill team. We call ourselves the *Wide Awake Posse*. These niggas will be ready to do whatever, *whenever*, for me." Two Guns Up motioned with his hands as if he was performing at a rap concert.

"So gather these dudes up, then we'll move out tomorrow night on his ass," Lex said. He gave Two Guns Up a pound with his fist, then proceeded back toward his area of the block.

For the next several hours, Two Guns Up rounded up his elite team of gangsters. Ill Bill was his right hand man, about 5'10", 195 pounds. Bill was brown skinned and was believed to be the first person in the city to bust his hammer at the police.

His other homie was Cookie Man. Cookie Man stood 5'8",

165 pounds with a dark skin complexion. Cookie Man was a member of the elite group and was about his money. He spent long days and nights on the block, serving fiends, rain, sleet, hail or snow, he was outside.

Last but not least, Trife. Trife was 6'2", 225 pounds, with a caramel complexion and was known for his intense thinking. Also by the way he maneuvered through the town. Trife was responsible for at least four of the city's most brutal murders, but no one could prove it, not even the police.

Two Guns Up got his name from the streets because every time he had beef, he would walk the streets with two guns in his waistline. Two Guns Up was the head of the notorious gang. He supplied his entire clique with crack cocaine. Two Guns Up explained every detail about the up and coming caper. He also said if he didn't make it out alive that Lex would take his position in the group. Two Guns Up promised once the heist was done that he would purchase the posse brand new 500 SL Mercedes Benzes. Plus Gucci link chains with diamond flooded medallions with the initials *W.A.* which stood for Wide Awake.

Ill Bill watched his partner in crime carefully before he spoke. Then he said, "I know you not talking about that skinny kid from up the block?"

"Yeah, son, he got a crazy lick that will put the whole team on the map." Two Guns Up explained his reason for wanting to join forces with Lex.

"If you feel comfortable with this, I guess I can't complain." Ill Bill turned around, looked at the other members of his posse, opened his hands then shrugged his shoulders with a raise of his eyebrow, as if to say, *What can I say.*

On the day of the heist, Lex and his best friend since grade school, a guy named Rich, met the most feared gang in the city at a discreet location in the Ville. They waited for the night to fall over the sunny afternoon and once the street lights came on, they headed out to Hamden.

Hamden was a nice suburban area just outside of the city where Sky spent most of his time. He also used the house for a stash spot. The Wide Awake Gang arrived at the location with their amo close by. Lex approached the house's door with his semi automatic tucked under his armpit. He knocked on the door and waited for Sky to answer.

When Sky opened the door, the whole clique barged inside of the three-bedroom house with their guns in the air. Two Guns Up was up for stuff like that, so he made his way to the front of the posse and yelled, "You know what it is, ma'fucka." But little did they know that Sky had two Mexicans, straight out of Mexico, that were armed with double barreled pump shot guns with pistol grip handles laying in the cut. The two Mexicans opened fire on the young men. The Wide Awake Posse returned a series of shots as well. The gunplay went on for twenty minutes. The notorious crew prevailed that night, but amongst the body count was Two Guns Up. He was shot in the head from the word *go*. Lex made out with fifteen bricks of uncut raw heroin and he kept Two Guns Up's promise to the group. He purchased them all new Benzes and Gucci link chains with diamond flooded medallions with the crew's initials, W.A., on them.

For the next twenty-four months, the elite group of men terrorized the entire city with drugs, murder and mayhem. They extended their activities to Fair Haven. Fair Haven was a town that bordered New Haven. It was also known for its murder rate, drugs, dope fiends, and Hispanics. Lex decided to take over the area by supplying it with heroin. He set up shop on James Street. Now that Lex was the head of the Wide Awake

Gang, whatever he said, went. If someone was late paying a bill or tried to interfere with his business, he would order them killed. Lex kept his best friend, Rich, by his side. He even named him underboss of the crew. Ill Bill made first lieutenant and Cookie Man was awarded the lieutenant spot in Fair Haven. Trife he kept close to him because he knew Trife was very brutal and dangerous, plus Trife was his number one hit man. Lex used him to protect Rich in the Ville and he was Cookie Man's protection in Fair Haven. Trife kept rival crews and up and coming stick up kids intimidated by his reputation.

Chapter 2

Out in West Haven, Lex and Rich arrived at Lex's townhouse. Lex opened his two car garage by remote control from the inside of his Jeep as they pulled up the driveway. Rich held the 4.6 steady, carefully steering the truck inside the garage door and parking it next to Lex's other car, a drop top 645.1 B.M.W. The duo exited the Range Rover, then entered the fully furnished two bedroom townhouse which was equipped with two baths and a built in moon roof. Sahara exited the master bedroom and jumped into Lex's arms. She gave him a kiss on his lips then asked, "Hi, Boo, where have you been?" Then she slid down Lex's tall and lanky body.

"What did I do to deserve that?" Lex stood in amazement.

Rich proceeded to the living room and turned on the 100 inch plasma screen T.V. by the remote control. "What channel does the game come on?" He flopped down on the soft Italian leather sofa and relaxed.

"What's popping baby?" Lex asked as he walked inside of his bedroom, totally ignoring Rich's question.

"You don't remember what day it is?" Sahara wiggled her neck, placed her hand on her hip, then balled her nose up.

Lex sat on his king size bed then looked into space, trying

to check his short-term memory bank. When he came back from his out of space mission, he remembered, "Oh, it's our anniversary."

"*Yes*, and I know you're taking me to the Club Diamonds. Everybody and their mother will be there," Sahara explained. She sat on the edge of the bed beside Lex, then she continued, "It's the grand opening. I know you're going to show me off." Sahara sat in Lex's lap, nibbled on his earlobe and whispered, "Do you feel like fucking?"

Lex unzipped his jeans, pulled them down to his knees, pulled Sahara's panties to the side then rammed himself inside of her.

"Ahhh, oh, don't stop, baby," Sahara moaned as she grinded down on Lex's brick hard dick until he touched her G-spot, then she lifted herself back up. "Come for me, baby, please, come for me," she yelled.

"I'm cumming. I'm cumming, baby," Lex informed her that it was time for him to explode like a time bomb.

Sahara bounced up and down like a bull rider. She gripped Lex's back, then bit the nape of his neck. She squirted her juices all over Lex's stomach. "I'm cumming."

Lex seemed excited. Sahara placed her mouth on his magic stick, then she drank his thick creamy juice, like a McDonald's milkshake.

"Damn, baby, you know you're the only man that ever made me cum," Sahara shared. She wiped Lex's wand with a hot bath towel, then he pulled his jeans back up and proceeded back into the living room with Rich.

"Damn, son, don't make so much noise next time," Rich joked. He lit a blunt.

"Yo, who is this nigga that owns Club Diamonds?" Lex asked. He took a seat next to Rich and grabbed the cigar filled with purple haze weed.

"This kid name Unique." Rich looked at his partner then continued. "He just came home from the feds. He did like 10 joints in the belly." Rich accepted the blunt, took three quick hits, then passed it back to Lex.

"Where this nigga from?" Lex questioned. He inhaled the weed smoke and held in his lungs for five seconds before he blew it out.

"I think this nigga is from the hill, but he used to get money all over," Rich explained that Unique was about his B.I. He watched his friend then with a confused look on his face, he asked, "Why?"

"Oh, nothing. Sahara wanted to go there tonight," Lex said. He checked the messages on his home answering machine.

Rich followed behind him and said calmly, "So we swinging through there then?"

"I don't see why not," Lex answered. He continued checking his messages. He looked at Rich, shrugged his shoulders, and spread his arms as if to say, *what*?

Sahara sat on the edge of the bed and scrolled through her T Mobile sidekick until she came across the initials S.U.M., then she pressed send.

Ring. Ring. Ring.

"Hello," Summer answered as she sat in a hot tub of bubble bath water.

"What's up girl?" Sahara asked. She searched through her Louis Vuitton bags for her purple Victoria Secret underwear, and before Summer could answer, Sahara continued, "I know you going to Club Diamonds tonight?"

"Yeah, girl, I heard that this nigga named Unique owns the club." Summer pulled the stopper from the drain of the tub. Then she wrapped her Ralph Lauren purple label towel around her thick frame. Summer resembled the singer Sunshine Anderson. Summer was 5'5", 140 pounds with a dark skinned complexion. She had long, silky black hair with blonde streaks. She proceeded to her bedroom. Her towel clinched to her 40 inch hips and her apple shaped butt when she walked.

"So, I know you coming through to pick a bitch up. I'm not trying to drive." Sahara made sure she had a ride for the night.

"You know I got ya. As long as you're driving next week." Summer rubbed her body down with Chanel Allure lotion, then she continued, "I'll holla at you later. I got a date with Ferrari."

"Ferrari?" Sahara sounded surprised, then she complimented, "that's what I'm talking about. Now you playing in the major leagues."

"You know how I do, it's all about the hustle," Summer reminded her friend how she ran her life, then she added, "Call Boosie and Pumpkin and ask them are they going to the club." When Sahara said okay Summer ended the call.

Sahara and Summer belonged to an all-girl motorcycle club that consisted of seven members. Sahara and Summer were the closest out of the seven girls. They almost always hung out with Pumpkin and Boosie. They called themselves *The Elm City Angels*. They all rode Suzuki 1100s and every time they cruised the town, the team of women wore outfits that matched the color of their bikes. Each girl had a self portrait of themselves painted on their motorcycle.

Sahara was the prettiest of the angels, while Summer and Boosie were the flyest out of the clique. Whenever a new line of exclusive designer fashion came out, they had it. Then there was Pumpkin. She went both ways, male or female. One would say she was gay, but she preferred you call her bi-curious.

Pumpkin was the girl out of the posse that would bust her gun and get money in the streets by serving marijuana heads hydro and purple haze mixed. She called it "Hyper."

Sahara was excited about her anniversary and going to the club so she called Pumpkin.

Ring. Ring.

"What's up?" Pumpkin answered her Nextel phone as she sat in her red Acura T.L. stuck in traffic.

"Where are you?" Sahara questioned. She pulled up her Chanel sweats, then wiggled her waist and hips to get them over her butt.

"I'm on the highway. I'm coming from New York." Pumpkin looked at her watch, checked the time and then continued. "I'll call you back in a half hour."

"Make sure you get at me." Sahara gazed in Lex's full-length mirror to see if she could see her bikini panty line then she ended the call.

• • •

"Yo, son, in the morning Soul is sending his man to pick me up." Lex had just ended the last message on his answering machine.

"What for?" Rich asked his boss. He looked dazed from the weed he and Lex smoked earlier.

"Maybe he wants to discuss this 950 thousand I want to spend." Lex reminded his underboss that he was going to cop twenty bricks of heroin.

"Let's go get some grub from Mother's Kitchen," Rich suggested. He had a taste for some Jamaican food. He picked up the keys to the Range Rover and proceeded out the door.

"That's a good idea. Just let me holla at Sahara before we bounce," Lex said. He entered inside of his bedroom and looked at Sahara. The devil appeared in his eyes as he questioned, "Where you going?"

"Me and Pumpkin abouts to hang out," Sahara responded as she put lip gloss around her lips.

"You be hanging out with them bum ass bitches too much," Lex barked. He gazed at his girlfriend with a jealous look on his face, then he continued, "I'm abouts to go to New Haven anyway and get something to eat."

"Oh, and you don't have to worry about taking me to the club. I'm going with Pumpkin and them. Then we can hook up at the club like we used to," Sahara explained, then kissed Lex on his cheek.

"Ahight, I'm out." Lex proceeded out of the bedroom, then he and Rich left the house.

Ring. Ring. Ring.

"Hello," Sahara answered her cell phone.

"I'm almost on your block, so get ready to open the door," Pumpkin spoke calmly though her phone. Pumpkin traveled up Lex's street, parked, then proceeded up the driveway. She turned and aimed her car alarm directly at her car, then pressed the lock button. She entered through the already opened door and said, "Girl, let me tell you, the traffic out there was murder." Pumpkin flopped down into the sofa and asked, "What's up for tonight?"

"I'm trying to go to this club out in West Ville. It used to be the Celebrities Club," Sahara enunciated.

"Yeah, I heard that Unique owns it," Pumpkin stated as she watched her partner, then she continued, "It's supposed to be some welcome home party."

"I don't know who this dude is though." Sahara looked confused as she sat next to Pumpkin on the sofa.

"You'll remember him if you see him. He used to drive a burgundy 420 Mercedes Benz. The one with the buggie head lights, back in the day." Pumpkin tried to help Sahara with her short term memory. Then she continued, "He got a new silver Lexus 430 with chrome B.B.S. rims now."

"I think I know who you talking about," Sahara slowly regained her memory. Then suggested, "Let's go to New Haven to see Chanda." Chanda was another member of the Angels with chinky eyes, Indian colored skin, 5'2", 125 pounds, and long silky black hair.

"Ahight, let's be out," Pumpkin agreed. Then the duo exited the townhouse, jumped into Pumpkin's Acura and proceeded to New Haven.

Chapter 3

Meanwhile, out in Brandford, a town outside of New Haven, Ill Bill along with the other members of the Wide Awake Posse carried out Lex's orders. The notorious gang dumped a garbage bag filled with the remains of Squirrel's body and cement bricks over the bridge into the river. The trio jumped back inside of their fifteen-passenger club van and proceeded in the direction of Elm City. They weaved in and out of traffic until they arrived in front of Rich's headquarters.

Trife sat low in the back passenger seat. He gazed at the other members, cleared his throat, then said, "Damn, these niggas ain't even here." Trife scanned the parking lot, then added, "I don't see the Range anywhere."

"I'll hit 'em direct connect," Ill Bill suggested. He picked up his Nextel cell phone, typed in the crew's code to alert the others that it was one of their members, then he waited for an answer.

Beep, beep, beep, beep.

"Yo, what up kid?" Lex answered. He sat low in the passenger seat. He turned the volume down to his eight-disk CD changer, then continued, "Where y'all at?"

"We in the Ville." Ill Bill spoke directly into the phone's

speaker. He questioned, "Where y'all niggas at?" Ill Bill took the phone a half of an inch from his mouth and waited for Lex to respond.

Lex and Rich passed two teenage women who stood at a bus stop on Norton Street. The females waved at the duo as they passed by. When they snapped out of their trance, Lex said, "We on our way to Mother's Kitchen. Why don't you's come through and have lunch?"

"One," Ill Bill said, then ended the call. Ill Bill looked at the others and said calmly, "Let's go meet them at Mother's Kitchen."

• • •

"Circle the block and see who those little bitches are." Lex pointed at the next block so Rich could circle the area.

Rich looked amazed at how thick the teenagers were. He pulled the SUV over and placed on his hazard lights, then hit the down button to the automatic window switch.

Lex motioned with his head and index finger in a *come here* motion.

The two young ladies approached the vehicle, looked inside and said at the same time, "Hi, where are y'all going?"

Rich leaned over the console and peeked out the window. He locked eyes with one of the girls then said, "Yo, Shortie, what's your name?"

"Tonya," the teen said, then she switched as she walked over to the driver side door. She leaned on the window.

Rich looked at Lex with the thought *we're fucking today* in his mind. He exited the truck and admired Tonya's tight caramel legs that poked out from the La Shai jean shorts she wore. Her outfit snugged her private area and showed the bottom of her butt cheeks. Rich said, "Damn, I know we getting up later?"

"It's up to my sister, I'm with her," Tonya shrugged her

shoulders and pointed in the direction of Lex and her sister.

Lex exited the truck as well. He leaned with his back against the luxury truck, then asked the sister, "What's your name?"

The seventeen-year-old girl looked at Lex up and down, then pulled his diamond flooded medallion from his shirt. She fumbled with it as it hung from his chain. Then she answered, "Monique." She looked at Lex then asked, "What does W.A. stand for?"

"That's my team's initials. We all got 'em," Lex informed her that he was the boss and that his team was rolling in the dough.

Monique stood in amazement with her legs snapped back inside her polo jeans. She asked suggestively, "Can we get up later?"

"Of course," Lex sounded excited. He tucked his chain back inside of his forest green Lacose shirt while Monique wrote her number down on a piece of paper.

Monique placed her hand on her hip, wiggled her head and said, "Make sure you don't lose my number."

"Don't worry, I won't." Lex assured her as he placed the number inside of his green and black Lacose socks, then stepped back inside of his Range Rover.

"Come here for a minute," Rich motioned with his head and hand. Tonya leaned into Rich with her arms folded. He gave her a hug to seal the date, then he gripped her butt cheeks and said, in a confident manner, "I hope you know when we get up later, it's on."

"You probably can't handle this anyway," Tonya smacked her lips. She walked back to where her sister stood.

Lex and Rich jumped back inside the 4.6, then proceeded to Mother's Kitchen. The duo arrived in front of the restaurant and noticed the crew's blue club van which indicated that the other members were inside. Rich and Lex entered the Jamaican spot and greeted the others with handshakes and half hugs. They all sat down at a five chair table. Lex ordered curry chicken and steak smothered in gravy for every one. The team of thugs chomped down on their lunch until they were full. After they were finished, the posse discussed up and coming business deals, and how they dismantled Squirrels body."

"How did everything go?" Lex questioned. He pulled himself closer to the table, folded his fist, then placed it on the bottom of his lip and the top of his chin.

Trife gave Lex a cold stare, colder than Alaska, then he enunciated, "We got rid of 'em."

"Good, good," Lex nodded, got up from the table, dug inside of his pocket, pulled out a knot of money. He unwrapped a hundred dollar bill and placed it on the table, then he continued, "Me and Rich are going to Club Diamonds tonight. Are you guys going?"

Ill Bill looked at Cookie Man and Trife then he said, "I'm good. I got things to take care of."

Cookie Man looked at the others, raised his eyebrow and stated, "Y'all know my M.O., plus I got to finish this package."

Trife looked at Rich and Lex, then smiled and said, "I'm in."

"Ahight, we'll come through and snatch you around eleven o'clock," Rich spoke as he picked his teeth with a toothpick.

They exited the store and they all went their separate ways.

• • •

Lex and Rich made their way to the Marriott Hotel. The duo rented a double room for a short stay. The double room consisted of two full sized beds and one bathroom. A short stay is when one only pays a fee for four hours and when your four hours are up, you have to check out.

Lex and Rich entered the room, looked around and decided

who was going to have which bed. Rich picked his cell phone up and punched in the two teenager's number.

Ring. Ring.

"Hello," Monique answered as she sat on her bed.

"What up?" Rich asked, then he questioned, "Where's Tonya?" He looked at Lex and nodded his head in approval.

"She's right beside me. Where your man at?" Monique asked before Tonya snatched the phone away from her.

Tonya got up from the bed and paced back and forth inside Monique's bedroom. Then she said, "What up, Boo?"

"I'm cooling trying to get up with you before it gets too late. A nigga gots to go out of town in the morning," Rich lied. He covered the phone's mouthpiece so Tonya couldn't hear his laughter. Then he continued, "I got a room, me and my man, so call a cab and come to the Marriott on Longwraf. I'll pay for it."

"Make sure you're out there. Give us like a half hour." Tonya assured that she was down for whatever.

A half hour had passed and the girls were waiting outside in a hot and smelly cab. Rich looked out his 7th floor window and spotted the taxi. He raced to the elevator and rode it down to the lobby. Rich scanned the parking lot to make sure he didn't see anyone he knew. He raced out the hotel doors and approached the cab driver. He gave him a crispy twenty dollar bill and said, "Keep the change, but be back here in three hours to pick them up and I got you."

Rich reached back inside of his pocket, peeled another twenty dollar bill out of his fat stack of folded up money and gave it to the driver. Rich entered the hotel with the girls close behind him. Once the trio entered the elevator, he pressed the number 7 button and gazed at Tonya and her sister. He looked at Monique and said, "Damn girl, I hope y'all into switching."

"I hope y'all niggas is packing?" Tonya laughed as she gave her sister a high-five.

They exited the elevator onto the 7th floor and walked towards Rich's room. Rich scanned his room card through the door lock and waited for the green light to appear, which indicated that the door was unlocked. They entered the room. Lex grabbed Monique, gave her a hug and nibbled on her neck. They wasted no time getting undressed.

Rich and Tonya laid on the other bed. Tonya pulled on Rich's rock hard dick and stared in amazement at his eight-inch wand. Tanya laid back on the bed, opened her legs and Rich got on top of her. He put her in the missionary position. Rich fumbled around her shaved pussy with the head of his dick until he found the entrance to her womb. He inserted himself into her and Tonya's eyes widened as she received Rich inside of her. Tonya pushed her knuckles into his stomach so he couldn't put his entire magic stick inside of her. With every stroke that Rich took, Tonya lost her breath and squirmed around on the bed. Rich gripped her tight so she couldn't move, then he said, "I told you my shit was the bomb."

"Fuck me, fuck me, don't ever stop," Tonya sounded excited. With tears in her eyes, she pulled Rich close to her by his neck.

• • •

"Damn, baby, yeah, just like that. Lex moaned as Monique licked and sucked on the head of his best friend. When his friend stood at full attention, Monique looked at Lex with her puppy dog eyes and said calmly, "What you waiting for? Put it in."

Lex got up from his reclined position and stood on the bed with his knees. With a kool-aid smile he said, "Yo, let me hit it from the back."

Monique balled up her nose like a piece of paper. She wiggled her neck and responded, "I don't be letting niggas tear my walls up."

Tonya watched her younger sister. She smacked her lips and in a sarcastic tone of voice she said, "Stop fronting, bitch, you know you love yourself some dick."

Monique positioned herself in the famous doggy style position, lowered her head and chest, arched her back with her butt poked out, and spread her butt cheeks with her fingers as Lex looked on amazed at how her thirty-six inch hips resembled an hour glass.

Lex inserted his member inside of Monique's young and tender womb and took long, slow strokes as if he were bumping and grinding at an R. Kelly concert. Each stroke that he took was timed perfectly with the beat. Lex's muscles got tighter as he tried to keep up with Monique's rhythm when his butt muscles gave out. He grabbed the bottom of his butt and his thigh and yelled, "Ahhhh, damn, I got a cramp!"

"Word, let me find out you can't handle it," Tonya joked as she lay on her back with her eyes in the back of her head. She smacked Rich's butt as he pumped in and out of her gushy stuff.

Rich, amazed by the sight of Monique's caramel complexion and butt, pulled suddenly out of Tonya, then he leapt onto the other bed. With his member hanging, he grabbed and squeezed Monique's butt. Totally ignoring his boss' pain with the famous kool-aid smile, he asked, "Let *me* put it in?"

Tonya watched the trio with a jealous look on her face. She felt left out so she joined the action as well. Rich wasted no time once he got the permission from Monique. He inserted his magic stick slowly inside of her neatly shaved box. She moaned, "Yeah, that's it, right there, baby."

Lex watched from the sideline, massaging his thighs. He

slowly regained his composure, then spread Tonya's legs. He played with her swollen clitoris with the tip of his member. Tonya grabbed Lex's pipe and gently guided it into her hole. He took slow careful strokes.

"Yes, yes, baby, you doing it, and doing it well," Tonya whispered in a sexy tone. She mimicked a song by L.L. Cool J.

Lex gazed back at his partner in crime, Rich. He winked his eye and smiled as if to say that that was part of his plan to get the girls to have an orgy. For the next two hours, the couples had hot fun sex. They switched back and forth, taking turns making one another climax.

"Damn, we got to do this again one day," Rich suggested as he looked out the hotel's window.

"That's what's up," Tonya responded. She put back on her jeans and sat on the edge of the bed.

Monique sat on Lex's leg and fumbled with his diamond necklace. She asked, "Where is your chain?"

Rich pulled his Gucci link chain from the inside of his shirt, then said, "Yo, the cab is out there." He tucked his chain back inside his shirt, then said, "Here's my number. Give us another call sometime."

"Ahight," Monique said. The girls switched as they walked toward the door, and before Monique opened the door, she added, "We had a great time. Thanks!" The sisters exited the hotel room, entered the elevator and proceeded to the cab.

Chapter 4

Meanwhile in the Hill neighborhood, Pumpkin and Sahara arrived in front of Pumpkin's three family house. The duo parked, exited the vehicle, then entered the two bedroom apartment. Pumpkin lived on the first floor. She rented the second and third floor apartments out to the government for families that were on section eight. With the money she received, she paid her mortgage and her car note.

"Damn, girl, I don't know what I'm going to wear tonight," Pumpkin thought out loud as she placed her keys on the counter.

"Where's Chanda?" Sahara questioned as she closed the apartment's door. She proceeded to sit down in the living room.

"Shit, I called her ass earlier and she was still over here." Pumpkin sounded exhausted. She took off her Nike Air Max sneakers then flopped down in the soft recliner chair to relax and massage her feet. "She's been having problems with Egypt, so she's been sleeping over here lately."

Sahara quickly changed the topic. "I'll probably wear my Prada jean suit, the acid wash jump off, with my gold bamboo Gucci heels."

"That sounds good." Pumpkin stared into space and pictured how Sahara's jeans fit around her thighs and butt, then with a smile she said, "Yeah, they do show your figure off."

"You better cut it out." Sahara smacked her lips then smiled. "What you wearing?" she asked Pumpkin.

"I'm thinking about putting my fat ass in my Dolce and Gabbana jeans, the ones with the big cuffs, and put on my Salvatore Farragamo sandals."

"Yeah, that'll be hot," Sahara commented on Pumpkin's idea.

Pumpkin watched her friend then she asked, "So how is you and Lex's relationship going?"

"It's good, and you know he can handle his own in the bedroom," Sahara responded. She got up and switched as she walked to the refrigerator.

"It's something about that nigga that I don't like," Pumpkin said. "And if he ever gets out of line, I'll bust a cap in his ass."

Sahara watched Pumpkin from the kitchen. She grabbed a Corona beer, opened it with a bottle opener, pranced back to the sofa, took a seat and said, "Stop talking like that. He's good to me. He treats me with respect." Sahara's voice sounded unconvincing.

"Shit, I see how he be trying to isolate you from everybody." Pumpkin wiggled her neck, then she added, "That's the first signs of an abusive nigga."

"Anyway," Sahara quickly ended the conversation, got up from the sofa and proceeded to the window. She peeked out of the mini blinds then continued, "that sounds like Chanda's car." The duo recognized the car stereo playing from outside.

Pumpkin questioned, "Is it her?"

"Yeah, it's her *and* Egypt," Sahara answered, as she opened the house's door. Then she added in a soft tone, "I think he's dropping her off."

Seconds later, Chanda entered the crib with her Louis Vuitton suitcase in tow. She smiled at Pumpkin, gave Saharah a hug and a peck on each one of her cheeks, then said in an upset manner, "I'm finished with him. The last thing I need is a dirty dick nigga."

"What happened?" Pumpkin questioned. She jumped up from the chair and snatched off Chanda's brand new Coach sunglasses to see if she had been abused. Then she asked, "Did that nigga hit you?"

"No, he didn't hit me, but that nasty ass nigga fucked trashy ass Tasha from Westville projects." Chanda expressed her anger. She wasn't a second class type of female. She proceeded to the living room area and continued, "So I might need a place to stay until I fill out the lease to a new apartment, if it's okay with you."

Pumpkin gazed at Saharah, glanced over at the suitcase, looked back at Chanda, smacked her lips and said in a sarcastic tone, "It looks like you already decided for me."

"Saharah, what's up girl?" Chanda asked. She flopped down on the soft sky blue sofa.

"Nothing. Just trying to keep my mind right with this school work and all," Saharah responded. She looked at the half empty beer bottle, took another sip of the Corona beer, then she continued. "You know, a bitch going to school, trying to get my B.A."

"Damn, you're a better bitch than me," Pumpkin joked, as she pranced to the fridge and got an ice cold Corona.

"So what's up with Lex?" Chanda questioned.

She gazed at Sahara, and before Sahara could respond, Pumpkin sucked her teeth, then commented, "All I know, if this nigga ever put his hands on her, word up on my unborn children, I'll do something to that boy."

"Why do you hate him so much?" Sahara asked. She shrugged her shoulders and tilted her head as if to say *why*?

"Sahara, you already know this crazy bitch is in love with your ass," Chanda reminded her if Pumpkin was given the opportunity, she would place Sahara in a bowl of chocolate and sop her up with a biscuit.

The trio joked and laughed, but Pumpkin quickly interrupted. "Okay, that's enough already."

Ring. Ring. Ring.

"Hello," Pumpkin answered her cell phone.

"Where you at?" Summer asked. She sat snuggled on the passenger side of Ferrari's pecan color Aston Martin Vanquish.

"Me, Sahara and Chanda are at my crib," Pumpkin said. She whispered to Sahara and Chanda with her mouth away from the phone, "It's Summer."

"So I'll have Ferrari drop me off there," Summer explained that she was on her way over.

"Ahight, we'll be here," Pumpkin said, then hung up the phone. She looked at Chanda and said, "You can put your things in the guest room."

"Who was Summer with?" Sahara asked. She looked at Pumpkin.

Pumpkin pulled from her ashtray a cigar full of her own *hyper* weed. She lit the blunt and took a pull. Calmly she said, "She's with Ferrari. She said she was on her way."

Minutes passed and the trio sat around passing the marijuana blunt around in a cipher. Chanda glanced at her friends, confused and dazed from the effects of the weed. She asked, "Did you hear that?"

"Hear what?" Pumpkin questioned. She glanced at Chanda and took two quick hits off of the perfectly rolled cigar.

Chanda got up, walked over to the window, peeped out of

the mini blinds and said, "Shit, I know I wasn't bugging. I know I heard something." Chanda raced to the door then opened it and continued, "It's Summer and come check out this nigga's ride." The other girls skipped to the front entrance. They stared in amazement at the big V-12 sports car.

"Call me later and we'll get up," Ferrari assured. He was feeling Summer. He popped the trunk of his car from his steering wheel allowing Summer to retrieve her shopping bags.

"Are you going to the club tonight?" Summer questioned, as she gathered her Macy's and Bloomingdale's bags. She switched her ass back to the front of the car, gazed at Ferrari, then she continued, "Because, I think I'm going.

"Yeah, I might check it out," Ferrari stated. He kissed her through the car's window, placed his car in drive, and before he drove off, he said, "Make sure you wear what I bought you."

"I will," Summer shouted as she blew him goodbye kisses. She turned and proceeded up the driveway.

When Summer entered through the door, Chanda grabbed Summer's shopping bags and asked, "What did he buy you?"

"I got a few outfits and some female gator boots," Summer said in a girly tone of voice as she sat down beside Saharah.

"So you still down for tonight?" Sahara asked as she admired the six-inch burgundy gator boots.

"Damn, girl, these shits are blazin' hot." Pumpkin examined the shoes. She placed her hand on the inside of them.

"Yeah, I'm still down, but who's driving?" Summer asked. The look on her face said *she* definitely wasn't.

"Shit, we'll pile up in my shit," Pumpkin suggested. Then a light bulb went off inside her head. When it went out, she continued, "We can all bust them other bitches in the head if we all wear our cowgirl hats and our matching bracelets."

"So how much did he spend on you?" Chanda questioned

Summer. The look in her eye said that she was tired of dealing with *in the way* hustlers like Egypt.

"Shit, two outfits and some boots. That's like twenty-five hundred dollars easy," Summer bragged.

Chanda gazed at Pumpkin, then she said, "That's the type of shit I'm talking about, furs in the winter and villas in the summer."

"Well, girl, let me tell you, you have to step your game up and get rid of that loser. He's only a nine to five nigga anyway." Summer schooled her buddy on the qualities of men.

"Well, tonight it's on," Chanda thought out loud. She entered into the other room to get ready and shower up for the big night.

Chapter 5

A cross town, Ferrari arrived at one of his many stash houses in a neighborhood called the Tre. The infamous neighborhood was known for its many gangs, high murder rate and drugs. Ferrari exited his vehicle then approached a group of men huddled around an exclusive pit bull fight.

One of the bystanders recorded the entire fight on his miniature Panasonic camcorder. He yelled with a wad of money in his other hand, "Yeah, that's it, now shake his ass, Ratzo."

"What's up, Tuffie?" Ferrari asked his right hand man. He patted Tuffie on the shoulder and asked, "How's Ratzo doing?"

"Get his ass, yeah, that's it, now bring this money home to daddy," Tuffie yelled. He totally ignored Ferrari's questions. Tuffie stared at his dog in amazement as he directed the camcorder up and close. When Ratzo locked on the other pit's eye and mouth, Ratzo bit down then shook the life out of the helpless pit bull. The helpless dog lay on his side, gasping for air.

The owner of the dying dog waved with his hand, then yelled, "That's enough, call your dog off."

Tuffie cut the camera off, squatted down, tapped the ground three quick times, then said, "That's enough Zo, come on." Ratzo unlocked from around the dog's eye and mouth as blood covered the grass and Ratzo's fur. Tuffie grabbed Ratzo's collar, then guided him away from the circle. He received thirty-five hundred dollars from the loser's owner, then answered Ferrari. "He looks good to me." Tuffie and Ferrari proceeded to the front of the project building with Ratzo in tow. Tuffie counted the money then said calmly, "So what's popping?"

"Shit, I'm cooling. By the way, what's the math on that issue?" Ferrari relaxed on the hood of his Aston Martin.

"We just finished one hundred thousand dollars worth." Tuffie assured his man that they were going to accomplish their quota. Ferrari reached down, patted Ratzo on the head, playfully rubbed his neck and mouth and stated, "That'a boy. Get that money, honey."

"What's popping tonight?" Tuffie questioned. He finished counting the money then rolled it up and placed it inside of his camera bag.

"I might hit this new club up called Diamonds," Ferrari explained. He watched his partner in crime then asked, "You going to check that jump off out or what?"

The duo was startled when two females came switching up the block. As they passed, Tuffie grabbed one of the lady's hand, pulled her close to him and said, "Damn, baby, you can't be walking through my hood and not speak."

"I spoke to y'all earlier," the lady explained as she pulled her hand away from him. Then she added with a sexy smile, "Hi, Ferrari, how are you doing?"

"What's up, baby?" Ferrari questioned as he admired the young lady's attire.

"What's good?" Tuffie asked, as he looked at the ladies.

The two young females proceeded to walk away, looked at Ferrari and Tuffie, then stated, "We'll get up later."

"Okay, we'll get up later, ahight," Tuffie assured the females that one day they'd get up. And the next time, they did, they'd be popping champagne bottles and living it up in a presidential suite.

Tuffie watched the girls as they switched back up the street. He looked at his right hand man and said, "Shit, we can definitely shut down that joint tonight 'cause a nigga don't got no problems bringing out my 96 drop."

"Well, I'm a blow across town," Ferrari said as he entered his big body Vanquish. He put the vehicle in drive, held up his index and middle fingers and added, "One," then drove away.

Tuffie was a Hispanic dude with a caramel complexion, cornbraids, 5'10", 185 pounds. He helped his partner Ferrari control the movement in the Tre. They supplied the entire neighborhood with ecstasy, heroin and cocaine. Although it was only two of them, they still were in control of the other crews. They infested the neighborhood with tons of money. They created this form of power which allowed the two kingpins enough voice and strength to be able to tell any member of the other teams to commit murder for them.

• • •

Back in West Haven, Lex and Rich arrived back at Lex's townhouse. Rich parked beside the B.M. as usual. The duo then exited the vehicle and entered inside of the pad. They sat down on the soft cream leather couches. Lex gazed at his homie, then reached under the entertainment system and grabbed the Play Station 2 videogame. He handed Rich one of the game's controllers and bragged, "You don't really want to see me in Soul Blade 2."

"What? Nigga bring it on." Rich accepted Lex's challenge.

"Let's play the best out of ten matches," Lex suggested. The look on his face said he was trying to get some spending change for the club later. Lex looked at his partner and stated, "Bet something."

"Fifty dollars," Rich yelled excitedly. He dug into his jean's pocket, pulled a fifty dollar bill from the top of his folded up money, rewrapped the rubber band back around the wad, placed it back in his pocket, then threw the crisped fifty dollar bill on the floor.

Lex reached inside of his pockets and unfolded *his* kind of paper. Only having one hundred dollar bills, he was forced to raise the bet to one hundred dollars. He threw the one hundred dollar bill on the floor and said, "A yard, fuck it, you can't see me anyway."

Rich dug back inside of his pocket, pulled another fifty dollar bill out and placed it next to his other bill that lay on the floor.

The two men played the game for hours. The duo went back and forth. Lex overcame Rich's pressure and won two hundred and fifty dollars from Rich. Rich glanced at his diamond flooded Jacob watch, then in a defeated manner said, "Damn, kid, it's almost that time to get ready for the club."

"Yeah, you right. I was getting in your shit anyways." Lex assured that if they continued playing that he'd win more money out of him. Lex and Rich proceeded to get ready for the club.

• • •

Hours passed and the Elm City Angels arrived in front of Club Diamonds. They sat four deep in Pumpkin's red Acura T.L. Pumpkin searched for a parking spot in the crowded parking lot.

Sahara looked out the front window in amazement, then she commented, "Shit, I haven't seen this many cars at a club since the old Alley Cat days."

Pumpkin's face lit up like a fourth of July firework show. When she noticed a car leaving from a closer parking space, she raced to the spot and parked. The ladies exited the car. Summer got out of the back seat, wiggled her jeans around her waist then the Angels proceeded to go inside the nightclub.

The girls walked side by side. They checked out each other's outfits. Chanda watched her buddies and said, "Shit, we going to hurt them bitches tonight."

The females entered Club Diamonds and paid the fee at the door. Pumpkin asked the dude that stood at the door with his arms folded, "How much to get in?"

"Fifteen dollars each," the security guard responded in a deep voice similar to Barry White, the R&B singer.

Pumpkin reached in the back pocket of her Dolce and Gabbana jeans, pulled three crispy twenty dollar bills out, and handed them over to the doorman. She held her index, middle, ring and pinky fingers out and said, "I'm paying for four."

Sahara glanced at her homies and said, "Damn, the security in here is crazy wild."

"This shit is crowded too," Summer looked around the club from a distance then continued. "Everybody and their mother is up in this place."

"Yeah, you right, shit let's check this mutha out then," Pumpkin suggested. The ladies mixed in with the crowd and walked in a single file line until they reached the girls' bathroom.

●　●　●

Ferrari arrived at Club Diamonds in his pecan Aston Martin with his right hand man in tow.

Tuffie drove his purple Porsche with the black interior. The duo found side-by-side parking spots, parked, exited their vehicles and entered the club. The men were escorted through the VIP line. They walked around the long line *and* security. They made their way through the crowd in the direction of the VIP section. Tuffie looked around, watched the crowd of people that danced on the dance floor and pointed. "There goes your little shortie and the rest of them motorcycle bitches."

Ferrari looked in the direction where Tuffie was pointing. Calmly he said, "Let's pull up on them chicks then."

Tuffie watched his buddy then followed behind Ferrari and whispered, "Hook me up with Sahara."

"Shit, I'll get you in the bedroom, but you got to get your own dick wet," Ferrari joked as they approached the ladies. Ferrari continued in a sexy tone of voice, "How are you ladies doing?"

"We good. We just got here. We trying to feel this whole vibe out," Summer stated. She looked at Ferrari, then glanced at Tuffie. Ferrari watched Summer, then looked over at Sahara. He lowered his head and whispered in Summer's ear, "My homeboy is digging your girl."

"Who?" Summer asked shocked from the announcement Ferrari had just made.

Ferrari pointed with a simple nod of his head and glanced at Sahara and murmured, "Her right there."

Summer pulled Sahara up and whispered inside of her ear, "I think his man wants to talk to you. You know them niggas getting mad money." Sahara watched her friend and thought, *All you ever think about is dollars and cents.*

Tuffie approached Sahara with his hand out. He grabbed her hand gently, kissed it and said, "My name is Tuffie."

"I'm Sahara." Sahara blushed.

"I already know. I've been a fan of yours for a while." Tuffie let Sahara know that he had been secretly in love with her for months. He then asked, "Do you have a man?"

"Unfortunately, I do," Sahara confirmed. The look on her face said *sorry, but I'm taken.*

"Who is this lucky man?" Tuffie asked. He raised his eyebrow.

Sahara looked back at Tuffie, then answered, "Lex."

"Lex, oh word." Tuffie nodded his head in approvement, looked at his man Ferrari, glanced back at her and continued, "Can I buy you a drink?"

"Well...well...,I'm waiting for him now," Sahara spoke hesitantly. No sooner than she could get those words from her mouth, Lex and Rich entered through the club's doors. They proceeded through the crowd.

Rich locked his eyes on the Elm City Angels, then tapped his partner in crime, "Ain't that Sahara and them dumb ass bitches?"

With an evil look in his eye, Lex watched his sweetheart then responded, "What the fuck is this bitch doing up in this dumb ass nigga's face?"

Trife followed close behind until he approached where the duo stood. He looked at his buddy and said, "Ain't that Sahara talking to Ferrari and Tuff?"

"Yeah, let's see what's up," Lex suggested, then the trio proceeded to where the Angels stood.

"What's popping?" Lex said with the devil in his eye. He approached Sahara, grabbed her by her arm and pulled her away from the crowd. He barked, "What you doing all up in this nigga's face?"

Sahara looked nervous. She had never seen Lex act the way he was acting. Then she responded, "It wasn't the way it looked."

Lex stared at Sahara and regained his composure. He

noticed the club's security guards then he assured, "Don't let me find out different."

Before Tuffie and Ferrari proceeded to the bar, Tuffie turned, screwed up his face, then said, "Easy, easy, playboy, that's my fault. I didn't know she was taken."

Trife watched his boss, then glanced at Tuffie and whispered, "Don't worry about it, bee."

Ferrari and Tuffie walked through the crowd, greeted Unique with a handshake and a hug, then Ferrari commented, "Damn, son, long time no hear from. I see you've been taking care of yourself."

"Ten joints in the system, shit, all niggas are able to do is work out and read." Unique was a fiend for good health, due to his stay in federal prison, then he admired Ferrari's jewels and said, "Shit, I see you been holding down your B.I."

"Well, you know, I'm trying to follow the path that was left for me." Ferrari laughed as he flashed his diamond watch.

Unique looked at Sahara and the others and questioned, "What happened over there?

"Jealous ass dudes, can't control their situation," Tuffie joked. He glanced at Unique then asked, "So this your joint?"

"Well, me and this Jew went half on it." Unique explained that Club Diamonds was a good investment for him, then he gazed at the bar and stated, "So what you guys drinking?" The trio then proceeded to the bar.

• • •

Pumpkin watched her buddy then gave Lex a cold stare and questioned, "You okay, Sahara?"

"Yeah, I'm okay," Sahara assured then walked with the rest of the Angles on their tour of the club.

Lex and the rest of his posse entered inside of the VIP section and popped bottles of champagne.

Trife watched his boss and underboss and said calmly, "Yo, kid, don't worry about them little dudes, they not on our level."

"This won't be the last time he see me," Lex enunciated and added with a sly grin, as if to say, *He* will have the last laugh.

Two hours had passed since the confrontation and the dee-jay ended the club when he announced, "This is the last song of the night, so you better grab that special someone and cuddle up."

Lex motioned with his head and index finger and said to Sahara, "Come here." Sahara switched over to her man, then in a sexy tone of voice she questioned, "You ready to go?"

"Yeah," Lex looked at the other members of his posse and stated, "Let's blow this joint." The Wide Awake Posse exited the club with Sahara in tow. They climbed inside of Lex's Range Rover then proceeded to West Haven.

• • •

Pumpkin and Chanda got inside of Pumpkin's car then headed for the diner. Tipsy from the champagne, Pumpkin looked at Chanda and said, "I hope Sahara is okay."

"She said she was good." Chanda remembered that she had spoken with Sahara before they departed.

• • •

Ferrari hopped inside of his Aston Martin with Summer snuggled low on the passenger side. Summer looked out the back window as they drove away and asked, "So where we going, to your place?"

Ferrari stared at Summer for a second then calmly stated, "Yeah."

• • •

The Wide Awake Posse arrived at Lex's crib. Lex and Sahara exited the truck then entered the house. Lex turned and said to

Rich and Trife, "Holla at me in the morning."

The duo exited the garage and proceeded back to New Haven. Lex entered through the door, locked it, walked into his bedroom, gazed at Sahara with the devil in his eye. He bit the bottom of his lip, grabbed her by her hair, then slapped her with the back of his hand repeatedly. Angrily he said, "Don't ever let me catch you talking to another nigga."

"No, baby, stop, please, stop!" Sahara screamed at the top of her lungs as she lay on the floor in the fetal position. She continued, "I'm sorry. I didn't mean to do it."

"You meant to do it, or you wouldn't have never done it." Lex barked. He stood over Sahara's helpless body, kicked her in the rib cage, then exited the room. He raced into the living room, sat on the couch, looked into the sky, grabbed his head and thought to himself, *Damn, what the fuck did I just do? I can't let her get me emotional.* He was brought back from his thought when he heard the cries that came from inside his bedroom. Lex got up from the couch, entered the room, picked Sahara up from the floor, hugged her as tight as he could, then cried, "I'm sorry, Boo, I'm sorry. I don't' know what came over me. Could you ever forgive me?"

Sahara reached around Lex's neck, hugged him tight, then said calmly, "You don't ever have to worry about me leaving you for another man. I love you."

Lex wiped her bloody nose, placed his thumb on her cheek, then wiped her tears. The two lovebirds made love for the next several hours, then fell sound asleep on the floor.